MW00916242

Shoved out i... ... cold, cruel world shivering
and naked by SeaMonkey Ink
A division of the sick mind of Grea Alexander

Genre: Historical Novel
Rating: Mature

Printed in the USA AKA the United States of
America or as I like to call it Uuusah

**Are YOU the bastard spawn of a Seamonkey?
Well, would you like to be?**

www.SeaMonkeyInk.com

Dedication

I would like to dedicate this book to myself, without whom none of this would have been possible. Without my tireless talent, faith, energy, effort, ability to exist in a fog of complete denial, questionable sanity and financial backing none of this would have been possible.   I truly am the wind beneath my crown.

I would also like to dedicate this book to the trees who so tirelessly and unwittingly and well.... involuntarily gave their lives to print this book because I prefer good old-fashioned paper books that I can actually hold in my hand and read.... or use as paper weights or tear out the pages of and clean my windows with (for that streak free shine) or hurl discus like at bad Seamonkeys.

And last but not least, I would like to dedicate this work to GOD who had the incredible sense of humor, mind-boggling ingenuity and questionable taste to create me and grant me what appears to the untrained eye to be a talent for stringing together such bizarre, twistedly amusing and vaguely disturbing thoughts in such a way as to actually create something semi-logical or at least decidedly nonsensical enough that it almost makes some sort of coherent sense but entertains and absorbs nonetheless.

Amarna Book I:
Book of Ida

A Historical Novella
By
Grea Alexander

Prologue

Thebes, Upper Egypt. 1274 B.C.

Queen Tuya did as she was bade by her father. She waited until she was completely alone, until not even her beloved son, Pharaoh Ramesses II, was present before she broke the seal of the first scroll.

For years she had wondered about what the scrolls, so carefully cared for and preserved by her father, contained, about what great secret he had safe-guarded so doggedly.

Still, now that she had been entrusted with their care, she was not so sure she should read them.

She stared down unseeingly at the neat rows of hieroglyphics, her mind drifting to the day her father had given the small chest of scrolls over to her. It was shortly before his death, not long after Ramesses had taken over the throne.

As he had lay on his sick bed, her father's handsome face had been so intense.

"Protect these," he had told her. "This

is my greatest gift to you: the knowledge of your past. Read them. Learn from them. Know that what Aten would have be will be regardless of implausibility, time or distance."

Even then, his grip on the chest had not loosened. It was only after he had drawn his last breath, a few hours later, that she was able to take the chest into her possession.

Snapping back to the present, Tuya re-rolled the scroll and tied the binding back into place. She set the first scroll down, went to the window and stared out of it.

At last she had the secrets of her family's shrouded past in her hands.

But did she really want to know?

She was, after all, no longer just Tuya, daughter of a soldier, but Tuya, once Queen of all of Egypt, mother of Ramesses II. What if the information contained in these parchments could cause her harm somehow? What if it illegitimatized Ramesses' succession to the throne?

Perhaps she should destroy them, she pondered, have them burned.

Her mind nearly set, Tuya hurried back to the chest, frantically returning the scrolls to its keeping. Gathering the chest in her arms she moved hurriedly towards the door.

She stopped just short of it. Her eyes drifted down to the chest.

If the scrolls *did* contain horrible secrets, perhaps others existed who knew what these secrets were. Would she not be better served by knowing what was contained within?

And what of her father? He had worked painstakingly for so many years to piece together their past - gathering accounts from diaries, witnesses, the words of her predecessors themselves. Who was she to dishonor her ancestors by burning their precious histories - potentially dangerous or not?

Her mind finally made up, Tuya returned the chest to the table.

She reopened the chest, stared at the set of scrolls for a time. Then sitting down at the table, she slowly re-released the binding of the first scroll.

I

Thebes, Upper Egypt. 1332 B.C.

One of Queen Ankhesenpaaten's hands lay on her stomach, the other gripping the arm of her seat so tightly that it had grown pale. Her face was drawn, wan. Dark circles ran under her eyes.

Idaten, Ankhesenpaaten's childhood playmate and favorite slave girl, worriedly applied kohl to Ankhe's eyes. She had already been at the task of beautifying the queen for quite some time now and found herself less than impressed by her results.

Standing back to judge her work, she sighed heavily, shaking her head.

"Why do you do this to me, Ankhe?" Ida said half to herself.

Ankhesenpaaten gave no sign of having heard her, of even having *seen* her though Ida stood directly in front of her.

Ida tried once again to improve Ankhe's pallid appearance - with little success. She put down the palate of powders and the brush, studied the queen intently for a long moment.

Ida was no fool. She did not doubt that should Ankhe appear in such a state, that it would be she who would pay the price. Still, what more was there for Ida to do?

Frustrated, Ida continued to study Ankhe's face as she pondered her predicament.

Perhaps food might help to bring some color back to the queen's cheeks.

"Esnai," Ida snapped at the new slave who was perfecting Ankhesenpaaten's wig, "go and get Queen Ankhesenpaaten her morning meal."

When the girl continued her work, unmoved by Ida's dictate, Ida's already brewing agitation turned quickly to anger. "Esnai, now!"

Suddenly having heard her name, Esnai paused in her work. She looked to Ida, awaited further instruction.

"Well go!" Ida ordered, making a shooing motion with her hands.

Esnai's expression mirrored her confusion. "Go where?" she asked.

Ida glared angrily at the girl for a long moment before walking swiftly around Ankhesenpaaten and slapping her.

The girl covered her injured cheek and scurried behind Batau, the well-seasoned slave at Ankhesenpaaten's feet.

Batau glared at Ida. "Ida," she reprimanded, "none of this is Esnai's fault." She turned now to Esnai, speaking loudly, slowly and clearly. "The Queen's morning meal."

Esnai nodded. She rose slowly, careful to stay out of Ida's reach as she backed out of the room.

Batau turned a hard glare upon Ida.

Ida, however, remained unapologetic.

"What?" Ida asked. "So much has happened just now. Pharaoh Akhenaten is dead, our Ankhe pregnant with his child and Smenkhkare's ridiculous mandate forcing us to abandon El-Amana.

"Now Ay and Horemheb are trying to groom Tutankh to become Pharaoh, are trying to force a marriage between he and Ankhe. How am I supposed to remember that that girl is a half-wit?"

"Ida, you know full well that Esnai is deaf in one ear."

"Excuse me, a cripple."

"Well, your memory for gossip certainly

seems to be faring well enough. Apologize when she returns."

Batau turned her attention to massaging oil into Ankhe's other foot.

"Why?" Ida pressed, defiant. "I didn't make her a cripple. She should learn to listen."

Ida, smiling at her own cleverness, picked up the palate again. She turned back to the queen, dusted at the dark rings.

"Mark my words, girl," Batau warned, "One day your insolence will cost you dearly."

Batau shook her head. "As if the entire world is to blame for Horemheb forbidding Tutankhaten from seeing you anymore."

Ida spared Batau only a dismissive glance.

"It is for the best, Ida," Batau continued. "You are becoming a woman, with a woman's heart. You are already too attached to him as it stands.

"You wear the anklet he gave you as proudly as any peacock. You even disappeared with him during the last Nile Flood Feast. No one could find either of you for hours.

"That is not fitting behavior for the future Pharaoh nor for one of the Queen's slaves."

Ida's hand paused, her grip on the brush tightened to the point that her knuckles turned white. "From where did you hear that I was with Tutankh Nile Flood Feast?" she asked. "Esnai?"

Though Batau did not confirm her suspicions, Ida knew that it was she.

"Esnai has far too much ambition to ever be truly trustworthy," Ida said, wishing now that she had slapped the girl even harder.

"Tutankh may well mean everything he has said to you. I have seen with my own eyes that his affections for you are indeed genuine and that the two of you have been almost inseparable from the very beginning.

"But Ida, you must understand that his duty will not allow this no matter how much he may want it to be so.

"He is still a child, Ida. His will is not his own."

Ida did not reply as she continued to makeup Ankhe's face, her own face set like stone.

Batau stood and grabbing Ida's forearm, turned her towards her. "When he becomes Pharaoh do you honestly believe they will allow you to be anything more to him than a servant, than just another plaything at the most?"

Ida trembled with fury, tears stinging her eyes.

Batau had no right.

"I know that right now you think I am just being spiteful, but Ida, you are *just* a slave girl, however favored you may be, a slave girl."

Ida pulled her arm away. "My father is of noble blood," she retorted, "blood every bit as noble as theirs. My grandfather's defeat in battle and enslavement does not alter that fact."

"You think you're the only slave here who can trace their lines back to royalty?" Batau asked, incredulous. "You think your grandfather was the first and only vassal ever to be put down by Pharaoh, stripped of his power and privilege and enslaved?"

Ida gave no reply though Batau could tell by the girl's wounded expression that her words had hit their mark.

Batau sighed. "I'm sorry for your family and for you, Ida. Truly I am. But as things stand now, of noble line or not, you are no higher than I or even Esnai.

"You are just a slave, and we are all the

---

same."

"I will never be like you," Ida retorted fiercely. "I will never bend and break my back until the day I die."

"Only time will tell," Batau replied wearily, her patience with the girl wearing thin. "Time will tell all.

"Still, for now, you are just another slave, and therefore, should consider yourself blessed if only to kiss the ground upon which Pharaoh has walked."

Ida shook her head defiantly though tears stung at her eyes.

"If you do not learn to bend," Batau counseled, "to play the game, you will break."

"I will *never* break," Ida swore vehemently.

"Won't you?

"How many times have I watched you locked in the confines, watched you released sobbing and wretched only to wind up in there again and again and again? How much more of that do you think you can take?"

A fleeting look of terror cracked through Ida's bravado.

The confines.

There was no punishment that terrified

her more than being locked in that small, dank, windowless box of a cell.

Batau's expression and tone gentled as her hearted softened towards the child.

"I will not lie to you," Batau said. "First affections are always the hardest to let go of, and you will probably never forget him, but Ida you must stop this self-deception."

Ida turned towards the window as she fought to control the tide of her emotions, to keep the bitter tears back. "Your warnings come too late, Batau."

Ankhesenpaaten bent forward suddenly. She groaned in pain.

Ida whirled to face her.

"Ida," Batau called stooping over Ankhesenpaaten, "the midwife!"

Ida ran from the room.

"Breathe, Ankhe," Batau told the queen.

Ankhe grabbed Batau's hand.

"May Taveret protect you and your baby," Batau said softly as she stroked Ankhe's back. "May Taveret protect you."

II

8 ½ years later.

"Mother, what's going on outside?" Heketya asked as she ran to Ankhesenpaaten's side.

Ida dashed to the window and peered out of it. There was a small procession of soldiers coming up the wide lane that led to the palace. Towards the front of the procession there was an elaborate golden palanquin, Tutankhaten's empty chariot just behind it.

Ankhesenpaaten was suddenly there next to Ida, Heketya holding tightly to her arm.

"They've killed him," Ankhesenpaaten cried angrily. "They've killed Pharaoh and there is no heir."

Ida placed a hand over Ankhe's mouth. She had, after all, vowed to protect the queen.

She looked around at the other servants in the room, then to Batau. Batau nodded and left the room.

Ida took Ankhe's arm and led her outside to the garden courtyard, close to the fountain where Horemheb and Ay's spies could not hear them.

Ankhesenpaaten was on the verge of tears now.

Ida watched her, unmoved by her display of emotion - knowing well that Ankhe's tears were of anger, for what would happen to her and her daughter now, not for Tutankhaten.

She wanted to scream at Ankhesenpaaten, shake her.

She took a step away from her instead.

"Tutankhaten came to me," Ankhe said. "He came to me and he told me that Ay and Horemheb had grown too powerful, that he planned to de-elevate their position and revert back to Aten."

Ankhe sighed heavily. "He was ready to take full charge of his reign. I could see the determination, the wisdom, the power of Aten strong within him."

"He would have made a brilliant Pharaoh," Ida said, "the likes of which Egypt had never seen before and will probably never see again."

"But now..." Ankhesenpaaten broke off. She shook her head as the tears spilled from her eyes. "Now we are at the mercy of our enemies."

Batau came out to them. "They're saying it was a fall from his chariot, that he hit his head," she told them.

"That's a lie," Ida said. "Tutankh was an expert chariots man, an exemplary hunter. He would not have just fallen off."

"Ay has ordered Esnai be taken down to the harem," Batau whispered. "Horemheb has ordered for Ida. I think they're planning to seize power."

Ankhesenpaaten turned to stare at the water as it spewed from the fountain, as she searched her mind for an answer.

"Ida," she said at length, "take word to Suppiluliuma."

"To the Hittites?" Batau asked.

"Tutankhaten has no heirs," Ida supplied, "and Suppiluliuma has many sons."

Ankhe nodded.

"Ask that he send one of his sons to me - to become my husband and continue the royal line," Ankhesenpaaten ordered.

"Don't you mean Prince Zannanza?" Ida asked, not bothering to hide her distaste.

Ankhesenpaaten slapped her.

Her chest heaving, Ankhe continued. "You do whatever it takes to get to King Suppiluliuma, and I do mean *whatever*."

Anger flashed in Ida's eyes though she held herself fast.

"I am, as always, your slave," Ida replied stiffly, "I shall do as you have commanded. However, with Tutankhaten dead, there will be no one left to protect you."

"Nor you," Ankhesenpaaten retorted pointedly. "*My* position at least will be enough to keep me and my daughter safe for the time being."

Their eyes locked in open hostility.

Ida had had enough. She couldn't wait to be rid of Ankhesenpaaten - even if only for a couple of weeks.

"They won't just let Ida go," Batau interjected.

"They will if they think I'm dead," Ida replied. "Galeno has told me of a potion that makes one appear to be so."

"Galeno will tell you anything to get between your thighs," Batau said.

"At least men still *want* to get between my thighs, Batau," Ida retorted.

"Stop your bickering," Ankhesenpaaten snapped, "and do as I have bidden." She reached into the small purse woven into her gown and handed Ida all of its contents.

Bowing rigidly to Ankhesenpaaten, Ida left to begin preparation for her death and for her journey to the land of the Hittites.

III

Ankhesenpaaten, Heketya, and Batau made a good showing of Ida's passing.

Esnai, emboldened by her arrogant rival's passing, had the gall to wear the traditional garb of a royal consort and stand just behind Ay.

As Ida's small procession came to the embalming chamber, Batau could have sworn she saw a small smile flicker across Esnai's face.

Horemheb's features, in contrast, were stony, wrathful - as though he would avenge himself upon death itself for stealing his desired consort away from him.

Powerful and powerless alike watched now as priests of Amun came to stand at the temple doors, as Ida's body disappeared inside.

Indifferent to the plight of a dead slave, the priests' faces remained completely expressionless as they waited for the bearers to come back out again.

Then, without a single word, the priests

---

retreated inside and the door closed.

It took but a couple of hours for the potent serum Galeno had given Ida to wear off.

Still, a couple of hours was all it took. A priest was already on top of her, taking his pleasure.

Though Ida screamed on the inside, she forced herself to be still, not to stiffen. Though she closed her eyes, she could not keep her tears from sliding down the side of her face.

Everyone thought they knew Ida.

They assumed she had lain with many men because many men wanted to lay with her.

They couldn't have been more wrong.

As at last the priest climbed off of her, she opened her eyes and stared up at the ceiling. Against all instinct, she fought to lie motionless as the priest righted himself.

Her mind drifted.

She thought of the Harvest Festival two summers past.

It was when everything had changed.

There had been a banquet at the palace. Most of the guests were drunk before the 2nd hour had passed. Ida, as usual, had managed to slip away before the greedy eyes and hands of the intoxicated aristocracy found her.

She liked at these times to walk through the royal rooms, to touch the beautiful, priceless things she would never own.

Ida had felt bolder that night than usual. Finding the passageway to the throne room completely empty, she had crept into the main state room.

In her naivety, she had been quite certain that no one was there, that no one would find her there.

She had sunk down onto Pharaoh's gilded chair, ran her hands along the gold, the embedded jewels. She had sighed in her contentment, the coolness of the metal feeling heavenly through her short semi-diaphanous dress.

She had pulled the formal wig that the servants were required to wear from her head.

Contrary to popular trend, Ida's hair fell all the way to her waist. Though she may not have had anything of any real value besides the anklet that Tutankh had given her, she made sure that her hair was the most beautiful in all of Egypt.

She spent many hours every day tending to it as she daydreamed, as she imagined that she was someone else, somewhere else - as she thought of the boy king whom she had been reduced to stealing rare, distant glimpses of for many years now.

Pulling her hair from behind her, she laid it over her shoulder. For a wig made of hair like hers, Egyptian aristocracy would pay gold enough to buy her freedom three times over – if only Ankhe would allow it.

Ida leaned back and closed her eyes.

Somehow, she managed to doze off. When she opened her eyes again, the moon was higher, illuminating the sky more intensely.

She listened. She could faintly hear the musicians playing and the loud, drunken laughter of the guests.

Her senses slowly returned as she continued to lay there.

Then, like a sudden splash of cold water, the realization came. She had been there much too long.

Hurriedly grabbing her wig, Ida rose from the chair.

She had barely managed two steps before she tripped over something and fell.

Her heart pounding in her chest, she had stared towards the throne, into the darkness.

Someone else was there.

She could see a shadow now - slowly separating itself from the side of Pharaoh's chair.

She blinked rapidly as her eyes adjusted to the darkness.

A man.

The figure moved towards her.

"You should be more careful of where you tred," his voice said.

He took her arm and helped her to rise.

"Are you alright?" he asked.

"Yes," she answered breathlessly, taking a few steps back.

What she had just done was treason and this man, whomever he was, knew it.

"I must be getting back to the banquet," she choked.

She turned.

"Wait," the shadowy man called.

Ida turned back to face him.

"You seem somehow familiar to me," he said. "What is your name?"

"Idaten," she answered.

"Ida," he whispered softly.

Strange though it was, the way he breathed her name sent a delicious quiver down her spine.

"I am head slave of Queen Ankhesenpaaten," she said.

"Why are you here, Idamun, head slave of Queen Ankhesenamun?" he asked softly.

Ida cursed herself silently. She had never gotten used to the name of Amun that Horemheb had forced upon Ankhesenpaaten and Tutankhaten, upon them all, in place of Aten.

"Yes," she said, "Queen Ankhesenamun."

The man waited.

"I...I ..." she stumbled.

Try as she might, Ida could not seem to think of a satisfactory lie, of even the slightest explanation for why she, a slave, was asleep in Pharaoh's chair.

Flustered, she lifted her chin in defiance.

Why was she even *trying* to explain?

She did not owe this strange man any explanation. He had as little right to be there as she.

Ida nodded. She would tell him as much if he dared press her.

"My lady will be wondering where I have gone off to," she said.

All at once, the moon seemed to be directly behind him. It illuminated her to him but only painted a bright halo around his body.

Ida squinted, searching for some clue as to his identity.

The man, for his part, silently bore her bold attempt at perusal.

He was wearing a long, pleated linen kilt, as the nobles wore, and expensive jewelry. His torso was lean and muscular. He was without a headdress and his hair, fashioned in the manner of a wig, hung just past his shoulders.

"You have grown even more beautiful with the years, Ida," he said softly.

He reached out and touched her hair. "And still just as proud and strange."

"You have me at a disadvantage," she replied. "Who, may I ask, are you?"

"I suppose that without my headdress and in the dark I would be quite difficult to recognize after so many years." He reached out both hands to her. "Come," he said.

She hesitated.

"You will be safe with me, Ida," he said.

Impulsively she had taken them - the action sending a frightening yet exciting tingle through her palms, a tingle which spread through the rest of her body.

Though she could not see his eyes, she could feel him staring at her in the darkness. She colored, her eyes fleeing to the floor.

She felt him moving her towards the balcony. When she looked up at him again, she had gasped. She was speechless.

It was *him*!

A strange delighted happiness spread through her chest.

She smiled. His eyes glowed in response, an answering grin upon his lips.

No, her mind screamed, breaking the spell. *Your Tutankh died 7 years ago. This man is a stranger. This man is Pharaoh.*

Her smile faded. Pulling her hands from his, she prostrated herself at his feet.

"Forgive me, great Pharaoh," she said, her voice trembling.

"Don't," he replied.

He stooped and, gently grasping her

arms, made her rise. "You have no need to prostrate yourself at my feet, Ida."

She looked into his eyes. They were so wise, so intense, so wistful as he gazed down at her.

She could still see her Tutankh in them - as if the last 7 years had never been. She was 11 again, a girl with the boy she would do anything for on the roof of the palace, watching the Nile waters swirl about the fields just before he had given her the anklet.

She pulled away from him and stepped out of his reach - the intensity, the vividness of her emotions terrifying her.

Tutankh's eyes became sad and weary. He looked down at his hands, then back up at her.

His brow furrowing, he turned and looked down into the garden courtyard.

The loneliness, the sadness in him was like a physical force. It reached out to her, encircled her, buried itself within her. She wanted nothing more at that moment than to take the terrible unhappiness away from him.

Against her better judgement, Ida slowly approached him, tentatively reached out and touched one of his shoulders.

He had tensed at first, relaxed but moments later as one of his hands covered hers. He had turned back to face her, his hand softly touching her face.

He drew closer to her, brushed her nose with his.

She closed her eyes, letting the sweet sensation of his nearness to her fill her.

His hands were on her waist now. She looked up at him. She saw her own turbulent emotions reflected back at her in his eyes.

He pulled her to him gently - his head lowering and his lips lightly brushing against hers.

She shivered, a tear trickling from her eye and him gently kissing the cheek down which the tear had fallen.

"Pharaoh!" they heard one of his personal guards call.

Ida was snapped back to reality.

She stepped back from him once more.

Going to the side of the gilded chair, he retrieved his headdress.

He glanced back at her once more. Then, putting on his headdress, he left.

The loud sound of the embalming

chamber door snapped Ida back to the present. She slid from the slab and stretched her stiff muscles. She looked down thoughtfully at her wrist and ran her fingers along the gold of her bracelet, an anklet she had years ago outgrown, that she never was without.

It had always had a strange effect upon her. It made her feel loved, protected, strong.

She began to pace.

She started when some time later the coded knock she and Galeno had agreed upon sounded at the door.

She went to it and opened it.

Galeno walked in and laid the girl down upon the slab. It was strange for Ida to look at her. The resemblance to her was quite uncanny.

Galeno gave Ida the dress and wig of a trader's wife.

Ida hurriedly stripped save for her tight sheer tunic and donned the trader woman's costume. Galeno, in turn, dressing the dead girl in Ida's clothing and wig.

"The caravan leaves from Cartunk at dawn," he told her.

She nodded.

Impulsively, she had hugged him. "You have been such a good friend to me, Galeno."

He smiled. "Just returning the favor, Ida. When they tried me for being with men, it was your testimony that spared me. I could have lost everything."

"I guess then that we have been good friends to each other."

He smiled sadly. "I suppose we have. I just don't want to lose you now, Ida."

"You won't. Not ever."

Galeno smiled again, more convincingly this time. If only he possessed the conviction of the young.

"My horse is at the east wall," he said. "Please be careful, Ida."

She kissed his cheek. "You sound as if you'll never see me again. I will return very soon."

"I will pray that you do."

IV

Only when Ida had joined the caravan and she was moving across the desert towards the Hittite land did the full force of what she knew descend upon her.

Tutankh was dead.

The grief hit her hard, consumed her - mercilessly, fiercely. Her thoughts became plagued with his quiet voice; his sweet, sad smile; his fragile, fleeting laughter; his gentle, comforting strength. She felt like she was dying inside, wanted very much for it to be so.

By the time she was before King Suppiluliuma her grief was embedded in her every glance, her every word, her every gesture. It made her beauty all the more remarkable.

Though King Suppiluliuma did not doubt her sincerity, he knew well that Ay and Horemheb were not to be trusted.

"I will send one of my scouts into Egypt to see if Pharaoh Tutankhamun has truly died," he said at length, "and if Queen Ankhesenamun or one of his harem is not with a suitable heir. If I find it so, I will send one of my sons to your Queen. But you Idamun must stay here."

"But Queen Ankhesenamun...." Ida began.

"It is the only way I will consent to send a son of mine into Egypt.

"I remember you from the Nubian banquet. You were very much favored by your Pharaoh.

"I have also heard tale that you are the favorite of Queen Ankhesenamun - very highly prized, well trusted. If this proves to be some sort of snare, Ankhesenamun will be more motivated to intercede if I have her much treasured pet."

Ida almost wanted to laugh. Ankhe would never let her go not because she loved her, but because she hated her and she wanted her to suffer.

He turned to the guards.

"Nacamakun, see that she is taken to the harem," he ordered.

A sturdy, dark brown man graced with unruly, raven black hair with gray streaks running from his temples and fierce black eyes nodded. He bowed to his king.

Without warning, the world began to tilt and swirl before Ida.

One of the King's sons, Prince Mursili II, caught her as she collapsed.

Shortly after the banquet that had seen Ida and Tutankh reunited, Queen Ankhesenpaaten had suggested that Pharaoh take Ida with him to the banquet in Nubia. It was a matter of impressing upon the Nubian King and the other great leaders who would be attending the vast wealth and superiority of Egypt to their own kingdoms.

Each year, the Pharaoh took with him his best finery; his bravest, most handsome soldiers; his most beautiful, efficient slaves. It was considered a great honor to be chosen to represent the best of Egyptia.

Ankhesenpaaten had brought Ida before Pharaoh. "Is she not beautiful enough?" Ankhe had asked him.

Tutankh had only glanced briefly at Ida.

He nodded. "She is more than beautiful enough."

"She is also an extraordinary dancer,"

Ankhesenpaaten had boasted, "not to mention a very well-trained and efficient servant."

"Mistress..." Ida had begun.

"Now Ida, you are more than qualified and you deserve this great honor.

"Some of the foreign nobles have even been known to take slave girls to wife," Ankhesenpaaten pressed. "Particularly with your pedigree..."

"I have no designs to be taken to wife by anyone, my Queen," Ida answered.

"Oh husband," Ankhesenpaaten went on ignoring Ida's lack of enthusiasm, "do not refuse me this chance to show off my beautiful little Ibis."

Tutankh looked at Ida again.

He turned to Ankhesenpaaten. "We leave at dawn. Have her prepared."

He left the room.

"My Queen, I don't think this is such a good idea. With the Pharaoh away, who will look after you and Heketya?"

Ankhesenpaaten kissed Ida's cheek and embraced her. "Ida, you are my truest, dearest, most loyal servant and I want the best for you," she said loudly. Then in a whisper, "Esnai has grown Ay's fangs. Horemheb's puppet himself will be accompanying Tutankh. Our Pharaoh will be hemmed in on all sides by vipers."

"Ay and Horemheb are up to an intrigue?" Ida asked.

"I can't be sure. They may try to ally the other kings against our Pharaoh. As a dancing girl, a servant, circulate through them, play the innocent fool, strain your ears so that you may hear any words meant to stir them against my brother-husband.

"You are the only one I can trust with his life, Ida. If you were of my own blood, I could not trust you more than I do now."

"Yes, mistress," Ida answered.

Ankhesenpaaten released her. She spoke clearly again. "As a token of my esteem please accept this ring."

Ankhesenpaaten pulled her most cherished ring, one given to her by her father Akhenaten, from her finger.

"I can not," Ida said.

"You must," Ankhesenpaaten said softly as she took one of Ida's hands and slid the ring upon her finger. "Should anything happen to me or Tutankh," she whispered, "I want you to ensure that the memory of the Amarna bloodline does not die as well."

Ankhesenpaaten kissed both of her cheeks. "Now prepare yourself for your journey," she said.

Ida bowed, dutifully obeyed.

Ida had had no contact with Tutankh the first night they had spent in camp.

He seemed to be slighting her, choosing instead to have Esnai serve him.

Ida had felt stung by this. Just a few nights prior he had been Tutankhaten again, the boy who had given her an anklet of which a slave girl was hardly worthy, who had looked at her as if the sun rose and set with her before the role of Pharaoh was placed upon him and he no longer was allowed to associate with slave girls.

Ida was still surprised that remembering affected her so deeply. She had long ago buried her feelings for him, the memories. She had assumed that they were dead, but ever since that night in the throne room, they had descended upon her mercilessly - like vultures upon a carcass.

She had been absently picking at her figs

when Esnai appeared at the entrance to the women's tent. Ida ignored her presence.

Esnai came to stand directly over her. "Pharaoh wishes you to dance for him," Esnai said in that sneering way she had taken to addressing the other slaves since she had found favor with Ay, as if she were their mistress instead of Ankhesenpaaten.

Ida gave no acknowledgment that she had heard anything Esnai had said.

Esnai repeated herself.

Ida continued to ignore her.

"Pharaoh will hear of your insolence," Esnai said storming away.

Ida offered the remainder of the figs to a group of young slave girls and rose. She pulled back her hair into a thick braid and weighted down the end with a beautifully adorned silver hair ornament - another gift from Ankhesenpaaten. She changed from her dress into a short tunic. She put kohl on her eyes, slipped on tiny dancing bells.

Ida had padded barefoot to the king's tent.

She found him staring absorbedly at a painting of the Nile. He did not even seem to hear the jingle of the bells as she moved.

She stood there uncertainly, not wanting to disturb his reverie.

"I've been thinking about you a great deal, Ida," he said at length. "About when we were children, before Ay forbid me to consort with slave girls."

He paused.

Ida had remained silent.

"Do you remember that last Nile flood feast when we snuck away to sit on the roof of the palace and watch the water rise in the fields?"

"Yes," she answered quietly.

"Do you remember what it was I said to you just before we heard Batau calling for you and you had to return?"

Ida swallowed past the lump in her throat. "Yes."

When he continued to remain silent she realized he meant for her to tell him.

She cleared her throat. "You said...you said that I was the most beautiful girl you had ever seen."

"And?"

"And that once you became Pharaoh you would pledge your love for me before all of

Egypt and take me to wife."

"You remember."

"It is not often slave girls receive such ardent declarations from their masters."

He turned around to face her. "I meant every word."

His expression was serious, his eyes probing. "I have never made such a proclamation to anyone but you."

She had to look away.

"We were just children then," she said.

He turned back to the paining for a time.

Ida looked back up at him.

After a long moment, he turned back to face her. "My Queen has told me you are an impressive dancer."

Ida could not stop the proud grin from lighting up her entire face. His eyes glowed in response.

"Dance for me, Ida," he said.

"Now? Without any music?" she asked.

He smiled, and he nodded.

Ida failed miserably to contain her laughter. "What would you like me to dance for you, Great Pharaoh?"

"Tutankh," he corrected, his eyes glowing in a way that made her heart thump loudly in her ears.

"What would you like for me to dance for you...Tutankh?" she repeated.

His gaze warmed her from head to toe.

Without warning, he took her hand and began to dance with her, whirling her around wildly as they used to do with they were children, before the world had become such a complicated place in which something as simple as their dancing together was clandestine.

They had fallen, laughing onto his makeshift bed.

They now lay on their backs.

"Aten, but I've missed you, Ida," he said smiling. "I'm glad to have you on my side."

Ida rolled onto her side to face him. "Pharaoh?"

Tutankh sat up and repositioned himself facing her. A sly smile spread across his face. "It has been ages since I have so enjoyed myself. Actually, I have not laughed like that since last I was with you.

"There's just something about you, Ida, that makes me feel free, as if I can tell you anything, can share anything with you."

Ida sat up. "That is not what you meant."

Tutankh laughed. "You are still very perceptive," he replied. "I have known Ankhesenpaaten for as long as I have been alive. I am also quite aware of Ay's and Horemheb's spies amongst us and I place my life in your hands - as I had my heart all those years ago."

"I shall do my best."

He reached out and gently cupped her cheek. "I know you will," he answered softly.

There it was again, this unnamable thing drawing them together.

"I never forgot you, Ida," he said huskily.

His lips tasted hers, gently, entreatingly.

Ida broke the kiss and stood abruptly. She turned her back to him.

He stood and came to stand behind her. Her breath caught. She did not dare turn around.

His hands were on her arms.

"Ida," he whispered, his lips brushing her ear lobe, his voice raw with emotion.

She trembled involuntarily.

"I've been so lonely for you, Ida," he whispered. "I want to bury myself in you, my precious jewel."

He softly kissed her earlobe. Her eyes fluttered closed.

"I want you so much, Ida," he sighed. "For all of these years I have dreamed of you, have longed for you. Your hold over me has not lessened with the passage of time."

His hands were sliding down her arms as his mouth moved along the tender flesh of her neck. "Let me love you."

Ida was weakening. She turned around to face him.

"We must not," she whispered breathlessly. "Ankhesenpaaten is like my sister, and if we are caught ..."

He put two fingers over her lips. "Tell me you don't want me," he said pulling her against him. "Tell me you don't feel this between us stronger than it's ever been, as if no time has passed. Tell me your heart belongs to another and I will bother you no more."

Ida could not.

He gazed into her eyes. "You are the only love I have ever known, Ida," he said huskily. "Love me."

His mouth was centimeters from hers.

"I can't," she whispered.

His head slowly drew back from her.

She had hurt him. She could see the pain in his eyes.

Her heart dropped to the floor.

He let her go and walked away from her, turned back to the paining.

Ida looked down, then to the entrance flap of the tent.

She stood there for a moment, uncertain.

She wanted to tell him that she had meant that she couldn't do *this*, not that she couldn't love him, that she *did* love him. She wanted to make him understand that there would be no going back for her if she made love with him, that her heart was greedy and it would never be able to go on as it had been if she gave in to it.

Instead, when he continued to ignore her presence, she left.

V

The noise level in the dancing girls' quarters was staggering. Ida had been silent, withdrawn since that night in Tutankh's tent. Even now she did not speak to anyone as she prepared herself.

One of the Nubian girls looked over Ida's modest dancing garb with disapproval. "That will not do," the girl said.

"Egyptian dance is more about movement than costume, about weaving a spell with the body than dazzling the eye with jewels," Ida replied defensively.

The Nubian shook her head. "I still say a little finery never hurts."

She went to one of the closets and pulled from it a long white dress. "Put this on," she said.

Ida stood glaring at the girl with her hands on her hips.

"Oh come on," the girl said laying the dress across her arms so that Ida could better see it. "None of the other girls have the flare to carry it off properly. Not to mention that the last girl who wore this dress won the heart of a sheik."

"I'm not looking to win the heart of anyone."

"Not even the heart of your handsome Pharaoh?"

Ida refused to give the girl the satisfaction of the effect her observation had upon her - though her cheeks burned.

The girl laughed knowingly. "You're probably right though. I can tell you don't need the dress to win his attentions."

Ida flushed.

"Yes," the girl pressed. "I see the way his eyes follow you when he thinks no one gives notice. The rich and the powerful never pay much attention to or even care what the slave sees."

The girl laughed again as she proffered the dress to Ida once more.

Impulsively, Ida had taken it from her and put it on.

When she looked in the mirror she hardly recognized herself. The dress was of linen. The bodice was sleeveless, tight, and cut low in front to show off the rich curves of her breasts. It had no back.

There were two sections to the skirt. One section ran in the back to the middle of her thighs, lengthwise. The other ran across the front of her, its edges just barely covering the edges of the back section. Whenever she moved, the sections separated, revealing the length of her firm thighs.

The front section was embroidered with gold thread in an intricate design, a fine sheer gold-colored material covering the wide waistband.

She looked like a queen.

Ida felt the girl loosening the braid that ran down her back. She let her.

The girl ruffled Ida's hair, letting the thick mane tumble wildly about her back and shoulders.

A gold armband slid up Ida's right arm. The anklet that Tutankh had given her when they were children served as a bracelet on the left. The ring Ankhe had given her adorned her finger.

The girl sat on the floor and put glass-jeweled rings onto Ida's toes.

The girl looked in the mirror at Ida who

seemed to be mesmerized by her own image. She laughed.

"What did I tell you?" she asked Ida. "You must keep it all."

"But I can not," Ida protested.

"You must," the girl insisted as she began gathering Ida's clothes. "It fits as though it were made for you."

"But..."

"It was my sister's. Now it is yours."

Ida didn't know what to say. When she turned around, the girl was gone.

Ida stalled for as long as she could before heading for the great hall.

When she arrived at the banquet, all eyes were upon her. She ignored them and began serving Tutankh. His eyes were the only ones that had any effect on her - a mixture of longing and pain when they fell upon her. They made her chest ache. They made her want to run back to the Dancing Girls' quarters and strip the dress from her body.

She was playing a dangerous game she knew, but she was unable to stop, addicted somehow to it. She could not deny the electricity that passed through her when their eyes met.

Though she forced herself to look at him as little as possible, her eyes could not seem to get enough of the sight of him.

One of the princes beside him inquired as to who she was, told Pharaoh that she belonged in the harem, not the slave quarters. Pharaoh barely even acknowledged the compliment, instead sinking even further into the dark mood that had been descending upon him since his last meeting with Ida.

Ida's dancing had been spellbinding. Her remarkable beauty coupled with her natural grace and sensuality brought every man in the room to her feet. They had offered Tutankh insane amounts of money and jewels and perfumes for her - enough to purchase 20 slave girls, support 10 wives.

Tutankh refused them with: "She is not my slave to sell." "She is property of my Queen. Only Ankhesenamun can sell her."

Ida pretended not to hear them as she resumed serving her Pharaoh.

As the liquor flowed, Faium, Horemheb's puppet, became freer. He began whispering in the ears of those around him of how weak the Pharaoh was, of how it was *his* master who truly ruled the kingdom.

As Ida walked past, he tried to grab her. Though she dodged him successfully, she knew it would soon be time for her to slip away. The rest of men were beginning to show signs of drunkenness as well.

Tutankh, however, was still on his first serving of beer. He was one of the few people there, besides herself and his personal guard, that chose not to indulge in the spirits.

The party was becoming rowdy, the other women loose. Ida discretely slipped away, back to the dancing girls' quarters.

There, she had removed the costume, carefully placing it and all of the jewelry, save the bracelet from Tutankh and the ring from Ankhesenpaaten, in the small trunk that held her belongings. She put back on her opaque undergarment. She sat down facing the mirror and began brushing her hair.

Ida heard the crash first.

She looked around the room. She was the only girl there.

Perhaps another of the girls had drunkenly stumbled back to another of the rooms to sleep off the liquor. At least that's what she told herself - though apprehension still gnawed at her.

She stood, hurriedly slipped on the short, semi-transparent dress she usually wore.

She refused to just sit there, an easy target. Brush in hand, she went to investigate. Slowly, she made her way down the corridor, peering into the other rooms as she went.

Suddenly, Ida was grabbed from behind, a male hand clasped tightly over her mouth.

He began dragging her back towards one of the beds.

Ida pressed the faux jewel on the brush's head and a blade shot out from the end of the handle. She jabbed it full force into her assailant's thigh.

The man cried out, let her go.

Ida dashed towards the door to the main hallway. She could hear the man stumbling behind her, cursing at her.

She flung open the door and dashed down the hall. Rounding the corner, she ran right smack into Pharaoh. His captain and lieutenant were with him.

"What is the meaning of this?" the lieutenant asked, catching her roughly by the arm.

Faium came limping down the corridor towards them. "Don't let her go," he slurred. "That bitch stabbed me."

Pharaoh looked from Faium to Ida. "Is this true?"

"Great Pharaoh, he attacked me," Ida answered.

"Did you attack her, Faium?" Pharaoh asked him.

"She told me to meet her in her quarters, then the little whore stabbed me."

"He lies," Ida said angrily. "I never asked him to my bed nor am I a whore"

"You lying harlot!" Faium exclaimed.

He raised his hand to strike her, Tutankh catching his hand before it could make contact with Ida's flesh.

"You're not going to let a slave get away with attacking a nobleman. Are you?" Faium demanded, incredulous.

"Ida is the property of our queen. When and if she is punished, it shall only be by my or the queen's edict," Tutankh answered.

"Oh. I see," Faium said looking from Pharaoh to Ida. "You're bedding the little tart yourself." He laughed sinisterly.

"I warn you to hold your tongue, Faium," Pharaoh said.

"You of all people, *Pharaoh* should know the penalty for adultery.

"Unless of course her cunt is so good you don't mind having your nose or ears cut off, public flogging, banishment, burning at the stake or being fed to wild animals for it."

"It is well that you know the punishment for adultery, but tell me Faium, do you know the punishment for heresy?" Tutankh asked.

"My master will not allow it," Faium said smugly.

"Perhaps you are right. Harsher. Gizom. Cut out Faium's tongue instead."

The two men grabbed Faium before he could back away.

"I'll take the girl to her quarters," Pharaoh said. "After you finish with Faium, send for Esnai. Instruct her that Ida is to receive twice the workload and no food for so long as we are here. She is to stay confined to her quarters unless specifically summoned."

"Yes, Great Pharaoh," Harsher and Gizom intoned. "As you have commanded, so it shall be."

They led Faium away, Faium yelling and fighting against them quite futilely.

Pharaoh took Ida's arm and escorted her back to her quarters. There she wretched her arm from his grasp.

"Why am I being punished for defending myself from rape?" she demanded.

He put two fingers over her mouth.

"You should have killed him," he said.

He gently pushed her hair back from her shoulder. "Still, no matter the provocation, it cannot be known that I chose the side of a slave over a noble."

"But I did nothing wrong," she answered in a sharp whisper.

"Which is why your punishment is for appearances only. I will summon you frequently.

"Then you shall eat. Then you shall rest."

"But Esnai -" Ida began

"I am well aware, as is everyone, that there is bad blood between you and she. Who would be judged more believable than your own enemy in regards to your penance.

"Trust me, Ida. She *will* gloat."

He touched her cheek briefly, then, without another word, he left.

VI

Ida was only vaguely aware of her surroundings.

"How long has she been unconscious?" Nacamakun asked the old slave woman who tended Ida.

"She has been ill since first she fainted, two days ago. She drifts in and out of fever, of consciousness." The woman was dabbing a cool, wet rag upon Ida's forehead as she spoke.

Nacamakun stood.

"I will check on her again when I return from my journey," he told the old woman. "While I am away, contact Prince Mursili. He will see to it that you have everything you need."

The woman nodded.

Ida drifted off again.

True to his word, Tutankh had summoned Ida often - though things remained tense between them. More often than not, he

---

was not there when she arrived. When he was there, he kept busy, kept his distance from her.

After their return to Egypt, he did not speak to her at all.

Ida was sitting on her bed, staring thoughtfully at the bracelet, gently running her forefinger over the gold when Batau entered the room.

"Ida," Batau called.

Ida looked up at her.

"Ankhe has called for you," Batau said.

"I'm sorry," Ida said. "I did not hear."

She rose and followed Batau to the queen's chambers.

"You have been very distracted these last weeks," Batau said. "You've hardly been eating."

"I'll try to do better," the girl answered absently.

"What's the matter, girl?"

"Nothing."

"Ida -"

Ida slipped hurriedly into Ankhe's chamber, before Batau could press her further.

Ankhe looked up at her.

"What's the matter with you lately, Ida?" Ankhe asked impatiently. "I have been calling for you."

"I'm sorry, my mistress," Ida answered. "I've been feeling ill."

"Come closer."

Ida did as she was bade.

"I want you to deliver this message to Tutankhaten for me," she whispered.

She softly touched Ida's face, let her hand trail in such a way that she was able to discretely slip a small note into Ida's bosom.

When Ida tried to leave, Ankhe discretely detained her.

"Not now," she whispered in Ida's ear. "Take it to his room at midnight, along with the sweets."

Ankhe moved away, the volume of her voice returning to normal.

"Take this to Pharaoh," she instructed, handing Ida a dish of sweets. "Sinic gave these to me in tribute."

Ida took them.

"And make sure you have some as well," the queen added. "I'm sure you'll find them quite enjoyable."

"Thank you, Great Queen," Ida replied, bowing low.

"Oh and one more thing before you go. See what you can do to dress up this gown," Ankhe said, gesturing to a gown strewn across her bed. "Sometimes I don't know why I even bother sending away to have them made, not when I never quite find them satisfactory until you've worked your magic upon them."

A small smile of bemusement spread across Ankhe's lips. "You should have been an exemplary seamstress.... were you not born a slave."

Ida went to the bed and examined the gown.

She picked it up. "I shall see what it is I can do," she replied.

"When I return from my outing, do come and sit with me a while," Ankhe said rising from her chair.

"Yes, mistress," Ida said bowing to her.

Ida had stood outside of the door to Pharaoh Tutankhaten's chamber for a time before she actually knocked.

"Enter," he said.

Ida hesitated before she pushed open the door.

"Shut it behind you," he ordered.

Ida pushed the door closed.

"Come," he said.

Ida went to him. She assumed the subservient position at his feet.

"All of the servants have gone. You may speak freely," he said.

She stood and reached into her bosom. She handed him the note.

He took it. He looked down at the tempting looking cakes.

"Are those for me?" he asked.

"Yes, Great Pharaoh," she said bowing her head and offering up the dish to him.

He picked one up and examined it.

"My taster has already retired," he said. "Do have one first."

"But it is from your queen."

"Do not argue with me, Idaten."

Ida stood and took one of the sweets. She put it into her mouth, Tutankh watching her chew and swallow it.

"How is it?" he asked after a time.

"It's delicious," she replied, "and I feel no ill effects."

"Have another," he said.

She looked uncertain.

"Go on," he prompted.

She took another one, ate it.

They waited a time more - to make sure it was safe.

"How do you feel now?" he asked.

"The same. Will you not have any?" she asked.

He put the one in his hand into his mouth. He opened the note as he chewed it and read. He swallowed it, then took up another of the delectable sweets.

He seemed lost in thought as he re-folded the note.

He looked at her. "You do still read do you not, Ida?" he asked.

"Yes, sire."

"And did you read this note?"

"No, Great Pharaoh, I did not."

"Why not?"

"It was not meant for my eyes."

"The last section concerns you," he said.

Ida gave no reaction.

"Come now," he pressed. "Aren't you the least bit interested in its contents?"

"I believe I already know what it says," she replied.

"Do you now?"

"I have been lapsing in my duty these last weeks."

"And why is that?"

Her eyes fled his.

"Do you not feel strangely now?" he asked her.

"My Pharaoh?" she asked returning her gaze to his.

"Do you notice any difference in yourself since you have entered this room?"

"I feel warm. My skin is tingling."

"Is it unpleasant?"

"No. It's quite the opposite."

He smiled. "According to this note, these sweets contain mandrake."

Ida dropped the dish, the remaining cakes sliding across the floor.

"I don't understand," she said.

"Mandrake is an aphrodisiac."

"I know what mandrake does," she snapped. "I just don't understand why Ankhe would -"

"Send them to me?

"After yet another stillbirth, the second of our two daughters, it was determined that

Ankhe's womb had to be removed in order to save her life. Did you know this?"

Ida nodded.

"It is Ankhe's hope that I might become nymphotic by the mandrake's properties and thus impregnate some woman, *any* woman, so that we may adopt the resulting child and thus continue the Amarna line."

"But I ate two cakes of it," she said.

"Mandrake will make you do nothing you would not have desired to do otherwise. It simply frees you of the fear that would stop you from doing so."

"It robs you of the ability to see the consequences," she answered sharply.

"What's the matter, Ida? Would it not please you to carry my child?" he asked.

When she did not answer, his expression soured. "How about to carry *Pharaoh's* child?"

Ida shook her head. She didn't know what to say, felt that whatever came forth would be wrong.

Pharaoh stood. He stepped down from his chair, Ida taking a couple of steps away from him.

"I'm curious as to what will happen

next," he said. "I want to know if the legends are true."

Tutankh reached out and softly ran his fingers down her arm.

Ida trembled, her eyes fluttering shut but a moment as she took another unsteady step backwards.

Melancholy crept into Tutankh's features.

He chuckled humorlessly. "Even drugged with mandrake you do not want me."

He stared down at her a moment more before he turned his back to her.

"Take the leave you so much desire," he ordered her.

Ida stood rooted.

He whirled back around and grabbing her arms, pulled her against him.

"Leave while you still can," he commanded between clinched teeth.

Though he let her go, she still could not move. Even as his lips came down solidly upon hers, forcing her back flat against the wall.

His hands grasped her face now, his body covering hers.

When at last he broke the kiss, his eyes

were wild with desire. Ida was breathless.

His mouth covered hers again, his tongue sliding between her lips. When it met hers, all of her bones melted. The mandrake induced heat turned to flame.

Ida found herself unable to think of anything but the man who was kissing her, whose warmth she could feel through her dress.

Her hands were on the sinewy muscles of his back, her mouth just as greedy as his. His need was pressed against her. One of his hands had found its way to her breast.

One of her legs lifted, her foot sliding down the back of his leg. He tasted the hollow of her throat as he repositioned himself - his throbbing organ pressed directly against hers.

Ida gasped, her hands tangling themselves in his hair. He whispered her name as his mouth explored the tender flesh of the side of her neck.

His hand slid down to the edge of her dress, sliding it up her thighs. Her hands began loosening his kilt.

When he thrust into her, she stifled her cry of pain. Tears slid from under her closed eyes, dampened her long lashes, but she could not stop this, did not want him to stop this.

When at last it was over, she clung to him and wept.

"Ida?" he asked stroking her hair.

She abruptly pushed him away and ran from the room.

Tutankh watched her retreating back in confusion.

He looked down, saw the crimson drops on the white of his kilt. He looked at the door again in shame.

Ida had been a virgin.

VII

The day was hot in King Suppiluliuma's palace. Though Ida's illness had not passed, it had lessened considerably.

She rose slowly and went to the window. She watched the children playing in the pool of water in the gardens below the citadel.

She sighed heavily.

The days here seemed long. It had been 4 days since she had awoken and still there had been no report from Egypt. She worried about Heketya. She wondered if she was safe, if she was even still alive.

"Miss," a voice said.

Ida turned.

It was Clizi, the old slave woman Prince Mursili had assigned to her.

"Yes, Clizi," Ida answered.

"I see that you are better."

Ida nodded. "Much. Thank you."

Clizi smiled. Noticing that some of Clizi's teeth were rotten, Ida redirected her gaze.

"Do you think it will be a boy or a girl?" the woman asked.

"Do I think who will be a boy or a girl?" Ida asked.

"The baby. Do you think it will be a boy or a girl?"

Ida still did not appear to comprehend what the woman was saying.

"Your baby," the woman stated - louder, slower. "Do you think your baby will be a boy or a girl?"

The color drained from Ida's face. "My baby?"

"You are with child."

"But that cannot be," Ida replied shaking her head.

"Oh, but it is," Clizi reassured her.

"You don't understand. I *can't* be pregnant."

"And why not?" the old woman asked. "Is something the matter with your womb?"

Ida shook her head.

"When was your last woman's time?" Clizi pressed.

Ida thought for a moment. "About three months ago," she answered quietly.

"Do you think the father will marry you or at the very least claim the child?" she asked.

"He can not."

"He's already married and cannot afford another wife or child," Clizi surmised, self-satisfied.

"He's dead," Ida whispered.

"That's too bad. Still you shouldn't fret, young one. You're a handsome enough woman. I'm sure you can find a man that will overlook your condition."

Clizi collected the dishes from the floor next to the bed and left the room.

Ida suddenly felt weak again. She went to the bed and sank down onto it.

She clasped the pillow to her chest. Then, she began to weep.

Ida could have let it all end there - the night she had run from Pharaoh's rooms.

It had become afterwards as though she and Tutankh were strangers.

For the next weeks, they neither saw each other alone nor spoke to each other. Sometimes Ida wanted to scream with the madness of it.

The night she had made up her mind to put an end to the silent, awkward tension between them, it had been raining. It was late and the lights had long since gone out all over the palace.

She had seen the light in his rooms still burning from across the courtyard.

Ida had raised her hand to knock, decided against it. She did not want to give him the chance to turn her away.

Instead, she had slowly pushed opened the door and stepped inside. He was sitting on his bed, reading a scroll.

His hair was damp. He must have gotten caught in the rain.

She closed the door behind her.

"I'm fine, Ekon," Tutankh called, not even looking up, a soft smile played on his lips. "You worry too much. See my wet clothes are drying." He gestured to a nearby chair.

When he did not hear the sound of the door opening again, he looked up.

Ida swallowed passed the lump in her throat and approached him.

She sat on the floor in front of him, took the subservient posture of those wishing an audience with him.

"You may speak," he commanded.

"I apologize for the other night," she said. "I had no right."

Remorse filled his eyes. "*You* had no right? It is I alone who should bear the brunt of shame, Ida."

"It was not your fault alone," Ida answered. "Know that I will keep this between us."

He came to his knees next to her. He took her head in his hands, holding her face so that her eyes looked into his.

"I hurt you," he said.

Ida looked away.

"I wasn't thinking," he whispered.

Ida pulled away and stood.

His words stung her. Worse still, she could see it in his eyes. He regretted making love to her.

Tears threatened. Tears she did not want him to see. She turned her back to him.

He grabbed her hand and bowed his head against it.

"I'm so sorry," he said in an emotion raw voice. "I was like an animal. I defiled you and I hurt you. I tore your innocence from you in a wave of mad lust. Please forgive me, Ida."

She turned back to him, knelt in front of him.

She reached out and cupped his face. His cheek was damp, as was her own.

"There is nothing to forgive," she answered. "I wanted that night. I've wanted it for a very long time now."

"But your first time shouldn't have..."

Her mouth upon his silenced him.

His eyes searched hers as she gently broke the kiss.

He stood wearily and went to the window. He sighed heavily. "I cannot be your friend Ida and I want more from you than just your flesh."

Ida stood.

He turned to face her. "Is this only lust, loneliness, pity or do you truly love me, Idaten?"

Ida was torn between the desire to flee and the longing to stay.

"All of Egypt loves you, Pharaoh," she answered at length.

"I asked if *you* love me."

"Of course I love you. You are my

master."

"Enough with the games, Ida. You know well that I ask not if you love me as a slave loves a master but as a woman loves a man."

Ida fought her heart. "It is forbidden. That night was forbidden. Even this is forbidden.

"We should not speak of such things. I should not even be here."

"Yet you are," Tutankh replied.

"I can no longer bear this, Ida. It's tearing me apart. Please. Just tell me the truth.

"Are you in love with Tutankhaten, the man you see before you stripped of all marks of Pharaoh, who is not your master but your servant, who has worshipped you since first his eyes and his heart could make distinction between man and woman, who gave you the anklet that now faithfully adorns your wrist, who would tempt death just for the chance to make love to you once more."

She stared at him silently for a long moment. She looked down at the ring Ankhe had given her, lightly ran the tip of her finger over it.

At length, feeling his impatient gaze burn through her, she looked back up at him.

She nodded shortly, her eyes fleeing back down to the ring.

He was before her now, his hands on her shoulders. She looked up into his eyes.

"I have wanted for an answer to that question for an eternity," he said softly. He gently stoked her hair. "It seems that I have loved you forever."

He delicately kissed her, before stepping back.

"I want all of you, Ida," he whispered huskily. "Your heart, your body, your soul."

"They are yours," she answered breathlessly.

Her eyes gazed into his as she slowly undressed herself. His did the same as he removed his kilt.

Their lips touched gently, probingly. Her body burned where the length of him melded against her.

He lifted her and carried her to the bed.

He was sweet, tender, lingering as he learned all of the secrets of her body. Ida had no shame with him. She touched him freely, answered his ancient signals with her own instinctive urges.

This time, as he entered her, he was slow, gentle. The ecstasy of it brought Ida to tears. She moved with him.

For many hours their lovemaking lasted, Ida even allowing herself to fall asleep in his arms.

In the morning, just as the first stirrings of life began in the palace, she finally slid into her own bed. When Batau would come to wake her, she would seem to have been there all night.

VIII

Ida felt it again, the strange gentle stirring in her stomach. Could it be their child?

She put her hand on her belly.

A child. A child conceived of purest love, forbidden love between a god-king and the lowliest of all servants, a slave. The only living child of Tutankhaten, the last true heir of the Amarna line.

Ida knew in her heart of hearts that it was Horemheb who had had her Pharaoh murdered. His wrath was terrible, his influence far reaching. If he ever found out that she was alive and carrying Tutankhaten's child....

There was a light knock on the door. Ida turned towards it.

Clizi.

Clizi ran to Ida excitedly. "Nacamakun has returned and held council with the king. He has agreed to send Prince Zannanza to your queen."

Ida half laughed, half cried in relief.

She had done it. She had saved Heketya. She might even be able to return to Egypt in time to say one last goodbye to Tutankh, to tell him that she carried his child before she fled forever from Horemheb's reach.

She hugged the old woman.

"There is to be a feast tonight in honor of Nacamakun's return and Prince Zannanza's departure. The king would be most pleased if you would come."

"Of course," Ida answered. "I can thank him before I return home."

"You will have time yet to thank him," Prince Mursili II interrupted from the door way.

Ida's smile faded. How long had he been standing there watching them?

"What do you mean I will have time yet?" she asked.

"My father has no plan to release you until my brother is safely installed as Pharaoh," Mursili replied.

"But that could be months," Ida protested.

"Indeed," Mursili agreed.

The joy fled from Ida. She sat down heavily upon a chair, her hand absently seeking out her stomach.

Mursili studied her for a long moment.

"My father shall be glad to know you have accepted his invitation," he said.

Ida looked up at him, her gaze stony. Mursili smirked before excusing himself from the room.

"Ladies," he said with a short nod.

Ida stared at the spot Mursili had abandoned long after he had gone, her thoughts and emotions in turmoil. It was only when Clizi spoke again that she remembered she was not alone.

"How long has the father been dead?" the old woman asked quietly.

Tears came to Ida's eyes as she turned her attention to the old woman. "He has yet even to be sealed in his tomb," she replied softly.

"The child is of the Pharaoh Tutankhamun, is it not?" Clizi half asked, half stated.

Ida was taken aback. "My baby is none of your business."

"I just..."

"Get out," Ida ordered. "Now!"

Clizi rose hurriedly and scurried from the room.

A powerful wave of grief washed over Ida, threatening to drown her.

She took up a knife from the table and held the point over her heart. Her hands shook. Though she tried to will herself to do it, her hands refused to obey her.

She dropped the knife instead, sent it skittering across the floor.

"Why Aten?" she demanded angrily. "Why have you taken him from me and left me behind with child?

"I can not do this. I can not do this."

She buried her head in her arms in despair. Heavy sobs shook her body until she had cried herself into a fitful sleep.

That evening, with Clizi's help, Ida made herself presentable and went down to the banquet. The great hall was noisy, bustling. King Suppiluliuma had even hired a band of gypsies to entertain the throng.

She found she could not force herself to stay amidst the merriment for long. It felt false to her - base, like a mockery of her grief.

She excused herself and came to sit at the end of the corridor, upon a window sill. She stared unseeingly down into the garden.

"Why are you weeping child?" a rough, scratchy voice asked.

Ida turned. It was an ancient gypsy woman.

"Leave me," Ida said.

The old woman did not heed her. "Your husband is with your god," she said. "The child you carry within you shall keep the Amarna line alive. His seed shall return Egypt to greatness."

"You know not of what you speak," Ida answered sharply. "There are still three left in the Amarna line, women who can still bare children."

"That may well be, but it is the child within *you* that holds the key to the future of all of Egypt.

"Protect him at all costs. Amongst his descendants shall spring the greatest Pharaoh Egypt has ever known and ever shall know. His name shall spread across the centuries, across the boundaries of time, and through him the Amarna line shall live eternal."

Ida laughed humorlessly. "The pharaoh is dead. A dead pharaoh cannot adopt a child into his line of descent or bond him from slavery.

"And do you really think that Ay or Horemheb will allow a threat to their play for power to become Pharaoh?

"They tried that once, with Tutankhaten, and they failed. He began to rebel against them. Do you honestly believe they would risk it again?

"And what of me? I am nothing more than a pregnant slave girl who can not even go back to Egypt, yet from me shall come the greatest god-king of Egyptian history?"

Ida laughed again. "Woman you are mad."

"Heed my words girl," the woman warned. "Though times are dark, they will get darker still. Guard the child well and tell no one of who his father is."

Ida was angry now. "Go old woman and take your prophecies to those who will pay you handsomely for them. I have nothing I can bear to part with."

"I do not seek payment. It is only an honor for me to have been in the presence of the mother of the greatest line of Amarnas that will ever exist," she bowed to Ida.

"You *can* do this, Idaten," she said when she rose. "Your one god is with you. Tutankhaten is with you."

A tear trickled from the corner of Ida's eye.

The old woman smiled softly, reaching out to gently touch the tear.

She turned and returned to the party.

Ida watched the woman's retreating back. She could hear the jingle of dancing girls' bells and beads and bangles. The sound transported her back to Heketya's 8th birthday celebration.

Most of Heketya's guests had been so drunk that they could barely see by that time Ida and the other girls performed their last dance of the night. Ankhe and Heketya had long since retired.

How Tutankh's steady gaze had warmed her.

They had been lovers for months now. He was becoming a Pharaoh in his own right, gradually seizing more and more power from the clutches of Ay and Horemheb.

He had refused to tear down the shrine of Aten and restore the priesthood of Amun. He had all but completely stopped the rebuilding of Amun's temples. He had even aspirations of returning the state back to monotheism as his father before him had, of changing his name back to Tutankhaten as it had originally been.

They were losing control of him.

Ida feared for him more and more each day. Yet, she could not help but be moved by his ever-growing wisdom and vigor, filled with love and pride.

Their lovemaking that night had been feverish. He was behind her, one of his hands stroking knowingly between her thighs as he thrust into her.

She could not contain a cry.

He had quickly cupped her cheek, turned her head so that his tongue could silence hers.

As they lay in his bed afterwards, Ida on top of him. Tutankh began to chuckle.

"What's so funny?" she asked.

"You," he answered.

She laughed softly. "Consider yourself complimented," she replied.

"Oh?" he asked gently flipping her under him. He slid himself against her.

She gasped loudly. He laughed.

"Promise yourself to me," he said rubbing himself against her.

"Tutankh," she gasped grasping his shoulders.

"Promise yourself to me," he repeated tasting her mouth.

She looked into his eyes. "I promise myself to you a thousand times and a thousand times again."

"And I to you," he answered as he stilled. "You know now that we are joined forever, don't you?"

Ida laughed. "That easily?"

"I am Pharaoh and I decree it so," Tutankh replied matter-of-factly.

"You know as well as I that neither the law nor society would recognize the marriage between a free man and a slave - especially not the Pharaoh and a slave. Not really anyway. At most it would be regarded as a concubinage."

"Alright, then I free you," he replied.

She laughed. "I am Ankhe's property, not yours. She was Queen before you were

Pharaoh."

"Oh," he sighed exaggeratedly. "What am I to do when even my own love does not recognize my power as Pharaoh?"

She smiled mischievously, one of her hands roaming to the length of him.

She began to stroke him. "Oh but Great Pharaoh, you are mistaken. If anyone knows and recognizes your great "powers", it is I."

He laughed deep within his throat. "Then *we* shall recognize our marriage then. *Aten* will."

Ida gazed at him for a long moment, her smile fading. "I love you, Tutankh," she said. "With all that I am, I love you."

"I know," he replied, "and I love you, my hidden queen, my Ida."

They kissed.

"And as a symbol of our union," he said reaching for a small box on the table beside the bed.

He opened the box and reached inside. Extracting an elaborate gold pin, he handed it over to her.

"Wear it always inside of your tunic," he said watching her expectantly.

Ida read the hieroglyphs. His name and

hers were inscribed upon it. All of Tutankhamun's royal wives had similar ones - though theirs were less remarkable than hers.

Inscribed upon on the back were the words: "My only true wife. My only true love."

She looked up at him. Tears of love had filled her eyes.

She had embraced him, then they had made love once more.

Ida glowed as she made her way back to her room, holding the pin tightly in her palm.

She went inside and began to undress.

She had stared at her naked body in the mirror, embraced herself as a warm smile spread across her face.

Tutankh. Her *husband.*

One of her hands slowly slid across her skin, her body tingling with just the memory of his body pressed against hers.

She set the pin on the shelf by the mirror and began to brush her tousled hair.

"My," a voice said from behind her, "don't you look smug."

Ida turned.

Batau.

"What are you doing in my room at this

hour?" Ida asked.

"It's almost dawn, Ida."

"Why are you here?" Ida repeated.

"I heard you, Ida. I was walking through the corridor to check on Ankhe and as I passed Tutankhaten's chamber I heard your voice cry out."

Ida opened her mouth to speak.

"Don't bother denying it," Batau snapped snatching the pin from the shelf. Though she could not read, she had seen the like before. She knew well what it was and what it meant.

She slapped Ida.

"You whore!" Batau accused. "How dare you lie with Ankhe's husband?! Do you not have enough with Galeno and Persuti?"

Ida cupped her injured cheek. "How dare *you* judge *me*!"

Batau threw the pin at her. "I always thought of you as my daughter. I always had a soft place in my heart for you, but no more!

"And Ankhe. Ankhe raised you above all others, treated you like a sister and this is how you repay her, by stealing her husband from her bed?!"

"Batau, I love him. I have always loved

him.

"And he loves me the same.

"If he were not Pharaoh *I* would be his one and only wife."

"Love does not excuse betrayal," Batau replied.

"Ankhe does not love him more than a friend. You know as well as I that since she lost her womb she hasn't been sharing his bed. She's been sleeping with Prince Zannanza."

Batau slapped Ida again.

Ida spun and fell to the floor with the force of it. She had to force herself to stay there lest she would rise and strike the old woman.

"I no longer see you, Idaten," Batau said. "Do you hear me? You are just another piece of rubbish, one of many."

Batau turned to leave

"Batau!" Ida called hurrying to her feet. "Please!"

Batau kept walking.

IX

"Idamun. ... Idamun....."

Ida looked up at the tall man-child who was calling her name.

Though she had seen him several times since she had arrived in Hattusa, she had never really *seen* him. He was handsome of face though lanky of frame. His coal black hair was even longer than hers, reaching almost to his knees. He couldn't be more than 3 years younger than she.

"Idaten," she corrected. "My name is Idaten. Ida."

"My mistake," he replied. "I was under the impression that all of your names were amended to Amun," he said.

"Not anymore," Ida replied.

"You were lost to us," the boy said, "in another world."

Ida stared at him expressionlessly.

"We have yet to be formerly introduced," he continued. "I am Prince Mursili II. Mursili they call me....amongst other things."

"I know who you are," she replied.

"My father has officially put you in my charge now. It would not do for you to starve to death in my care."

"I am not hungry," Ida answered.

"In your condition you *must* eat," he replied. "In fact, I insist."

"My condition?" Ida repeated.

"Clizi..."

"Is there anyone she hasn't told yet?" Ida asked, incredulous.

"Clizi only told me because it is her duty to. She told Nac because he might be suited to..."

Ida rose and tried to leave. He grabbed her arm.

"Boy or not, I am still Prince and you *will* show me all due respect."

"Forgive me, your highness," Ida replied. Though she struggled to contain her emotions, she still knew well her place. "I meant no disrespect. Truly, I did not. And I sincerely appreciate everything you, Nac and Clizi have done for me thus far -"

"But?"

"But it's just too soon." She smiled sadly. "You don't think I know it would be wise for me to accept Nac, that his support is a more than generous offer - far more than I deserve?"

She shook her head. "I haven't even *begun* to mourn."

"Mourn?" he replied. "You can mourn for the rest of your life if you like. This offer, however, is temporary - your pregnancy soon to be obvious to all.

"Nac may be far from young or rich but he does have rank, stability. He has a very healthy estate and an heir - not to mention the ear of the King.

"Nac wishes to marry soon. I would not dally long if I were in your shoes."

"I can not accept Nac or any other man of Hattusa – under any circumstances," Ida insisted. "Once Prince Zannanza becomes Pharaoh, I plan to return home."

"Then what?" he asked. "You think you or that child will *ever* be safe in Egypt?"

"I have friends, people who will help me start a new life away from the palace."

Mursili smirked cynically.

"As you will," he said. "You're making a serious mistake. But then it's yours to make isn't it?"

"It is," she replied evenly, though Mursili could all but feel the fire in her boiling towards the surface.

He nodded. "No one aside from Nac, Clizi and I know the paternity of your child and I plan on keeping it that way.

"So long as you remain in our land, and I draw breath, I promise that no harm will come to either you or your child.

"Neither of you will have anything to fear - not from my father, not from Zannanza and certainly not from Ay or Horemheb."

"I am honored to have your protection, Mighty Prince."

Mursili smirked. "I will leave you now, but I expect you to rejoin the banquet and eat well."

"As you have commanded," Ida replied with a bow.

She watched as the boy continued down the hall, away from the gathering, then returned to the banquet to do as she was bade.

Mursili found the old woman easily

enough. She was waiting for him in one of the lower alcoves.

Angrily Mursili grabbed the woman's arm and pulled her into one of the empty rooms. He shut the door behind them.

Alone, he pulled the wrap and wig from the woman's head and threw it to the ground.

"What are you doing here, witch?" he demanded.

The old woman laughed.

"Is that any way to greet your mother?" she asked. "Your father and his Babylonian whore may well have banished me from Hattusa but never forget that *I* am still Suppiluliuma's chief wife. *I* am still the one, true queen."

"Answer, woman."

"Can't a mother just want to visit her handsome son?" she asked reaching out a hand to stoke his face.

Mursili pushed her hand away. "Not when it may cost her her life or get her son banished."

"And who would dare turn me in?"

"That is not the point, mother. You know well how to reach me outside of the King's influence."

"I came to see the girl," the woman

admitted.

"The one who calls herself Ida?" Mursili asked.

The woman smiled. "You've seen it too, haven't you?" she taunted.

"Seen what?" he replied.

The woman laughed. "I knew it! Suppilu did not drive *all* of the "witches" from the citadel did he?"

"I am nothing like you."

"No? Do the gods Arinna & Telipinu not speak to you?"

"Only in my sleep," he relented, relieved to share the truth of who and what he was - if only for a moment.

"And does *he* know?"

"Of course not. Only Nacamakun knows... and you."

"How long has it been happening?" she asked.

"Since my 13ᵗʰ year."

The old woman nodded, considering. "You must never tell him – no matter what.

"Your future depends upon it.

"Suppilu will banish you like he did me....or perhaps even worse should you fail to see what it is he wishes you to see."

"I remember well what he did to you. I will not make the same mistake."

"Suppilu has already started down a road to ruin, one from which there is no return. He saw to that when he murdered his brother Tudhaliya and usurped the throne.

"Your visions in his hands will only bring you ruin. But in *your* hands, in your hands Mursili our kingdom might yet be saved from your father's fate."

"But how?" he asked.

"The girl, Mursili. You must protect the girl and her offspring at all costs. Her fate is tied to yours and to that of the Hittites. If her line falls, then so shall we."

Mursili stared at her for a long moment. "Just how far ahead have you seen?"

"I have seen shimmers, glimpses across the sands of times.

"Not all can be prevented, but if you protect her line, our kingdom will not only survive but thrive. And one day, when you are at your most vulnerable, she will protect *you.*"

"You lay too much at the feet of a 4th level Prince and an Egyptian slave girl, mother."

"It is not I, my son. It's the gods.

"They are with you, Mursili. Heed them."

She picked up the wig and wrap, replacing them on her head.

"I have lingered longer than I had intended," she said. "I believe in you, son. Never forget that."

She turned to leave.

"Mother, I-" he called.

She turned back to face him, smiled knowingly.

"I know, Mursili," she said. "I know."

X

The past. Ida lived more in the past now than she did in the present. Once again, as she lay in the tub, Clizi's kind and careful hands bathing her, her thoughts returned to Egypt.

Batau's heart had hardened towards Ida - from the night she had caught Ida with Tutankh onward.

They hardly spoke, even now as they prepared Ankhe for a luncheon with the other royal wives.

"I have noticed a rift between the two of you these past few days," Ankhe said pointedly. "What has happened?"

Neither of them spoke.

"Pharaoh has changed as well," Ankhe remarked in that strange sharp tone.

Ida forced herself to remain passive. "Has he?" she asked.

"Indeed. He has been going against Ay and Horemheb's wishes. He is also happier than I have seen him since he has become Pharaoh. He is as he was when he was a boy."

Neither of the other two women spoke.

"He's in love," Ankhe said. "He radiates with it. It gives him strength. The sadness, the loneliness is gone from him."

Ida glanced pointedly at Batau. Batau looked back down to her task.

"I know it is not one of his other wives. He doesn't even look at them. It is someone else."

Ankhe looked directly at Ida. Ida's face burned.

Ankhe's eyes fell next upon the bracelet then drifted back up to Ida's face.

"Batau," Ankhe said, "could you go with Esnai to pick up my new wig?"

"Yes, mistress," Batau said rising and leaving the room.

Ida watched Batau leave.

"This woman, whoever she is, makes him very happy. No one deserves to be happy more than Tutankh, do they Ida?"

"No," Ida answered softly.

"I must admit though that I am quite jealous," Ankhe continued steadily. "In all our years of marriage he has never touched me out of more than conjugal necessity, never in love or desire. After my womb was corrupted, he stopped touching me altogether."

She stood. "Have you heard anything, seen anything that might give you suspicion as to who she may be or even if it is a woman at all?"

The way Ankhe kept pressing the matter with her, the way she kept glaring at her, there was only one conclusion Ida could draw.

She knows.

Ida sank to her knees before Ankhe. Tears spilled from her eyes.

"You know something, Ida?" Ankhe asked, feigning ignorance.

"Please forgive me," Ida begged.

"Forgive you?"

"I know Batau has told you. You know well that I am the woman in question."

"You, Ida?" Ankhe asked though she did not sound surprised.

"Please don't send me away," Ida begged. "I can't let him go again. It would destroy us both."

"How romantic or should I say.....melodramatic!"

Ankhe laughed humorlessly. "Of

course I should have guessed long ago that things would turn out this way. Even when you were children you had this....unnatural attachment."

"I did not mean to betray you, Ankhe. You must believe me when I say I resisted as long as I could."

Ankhe walked away from her. She laughed that strange dry laugh again. "It was only an accident of birth that made him my husband. It's you he's always loved.

"Still, I can hardly fault him, Ida.

"I'm in love with you as well."

Ida stood slowly, her shock written all over her face.

Ankhe turned to face her. "Are you surprised to hear that I love you in that way?"

Ida didn't answer.

"I was never quite sure of how to approach you, could never quite figure out how to tell you."

She laughed dryly.

"Do you know we used to argue over you, Ida? Though he knew how I felt, he too refused to give you up.

"Almost anything else I have ever asked

of him, he has given me. But when it came to you..." she shook her head.

"I was so glad when he became Pharaoh. All I had to do was put the idea into Horemheb's head that he was becoming too attached to you, that you could be a threat to his control over Tutankh.

"Day after day, I drummed it in. Until finally Horemheb came around to my way of thinking.

"I had hoped time and absence would erase this thing from the both of your minds. But I guess I was wrong wasn't I, Ida?"

"How could you do such a thing?" Ida asked, her hurt badly constrained. "You of all people knew how we felt about each other."

"Felt or feel?"

"I *never* stopped loving him. Even when all I had was this bracelet and a few distant glimpses of him, my feelings for him didn't die. They could never."

Ankhe laughed dryly. "How sweet.

"And to think I was murderously jealous when Batau first told me of your little run in the other night - angry at the both of you. My fury, however, can not change the way you look at each other can it? My wrath can not expunge him from your heart?"

"No," Ida admitted quietly.

"And you're sure about that, Ida?" Ankhe pressed.

Ida did not reply, her apprehension beginning to rise. She knew well that look in Ankhe's eyes.

Ankhe laughed again. "How can this be?" she asked.

"I am Queen. I am chosen by the gods to rule. I am above all others, yet, this love, this great immovable unyielding passion should be denied me, should be instead bestowed upon a mere slave, a slave I myself love nonetheless - and with my own brother, my own husband."

She laughed even harder. "What a cruel hoax this is!"

Ankhe's mad laughter gradually subsided. She was silent for a time now as she studied Ida.

Finally, the queen spoke. "I will not sell you or send you away. What fun would that be for me?

"And I *will* keep what I know a secret, for now, for the love I once bore the two of you. But if anyone else should find out about your affair or any of mine for that matter, I will have you thrown to the crocodiles. Is that clear?"

"Yes, my queen," Ida replied, her terror continuing to rise as Ankhe slowly approached her.

Ankhe pressed her lips against Ida's, wrapped her arms around her and pressed the girl to her. When Ida pushed away, tears were in Ankhe's eyes.

Ankhe sneered at her. "We'll see just how much this "love" between you and my brother really means to you."

She signaled to her private guard.

Just as Ida turned, she felt a blow to the back of her head.

Then, nothing.

When at last Ida came to, it was very dark. She could hardly move, hardly breathe. The temperature was stifling.

Panic quickly set in. She began screaming, banging desperately against her prison.

"Help!" she cried though she struggled to breathe, tears pouring from her eyes, blurring her sight. "Let me out!"

She cried out over and over again - until her voice was barely above a hoarse whisper, until her hair and clothing were pasted to her body with sweat.

Now, exhausted, all she could do was sob.

"Giving up so soon?" a familiar voice asked.

Ankhe.

"Please let me out!" Ida sobbed pitifully. "Please have mercy!"

"I will free you....in time," Ankhe promised as she sank down next to the coffin, "when you've learned your lesson."

Ida groaned in despair. "Why are you doing this?!"

"You need to learn your place. Years of favor have made you disrespectful. You have taken my kindness for weakness."

"That's not true."

"Isn't it? Even now you are insolent."

"No," Ida sobbed loudly. "Please don't do this!"

"You won't stop seeing my husband. Fine. Just know that each and every time you do, you will end up here.

"You will never know when or where or for how long but know this. It *will* happen."

"My queen..." Ida begged.

"*Every.* Time," Ankhe repeated.

"I trust it goes without saying that you are to tell no one about this, about our special time together, especially not Pharaoh. If you do or even if I *suspect* you have, I'll have you buried alive in the desert, right here in your cozy little home away from home."

"I won't say anything," Ida promised. "Please just stop this. I've had enough."

"I'll decide when you've had enough." Ankhe rose, a smile of satisfaction on her face.

"Ankhe? Ankhe!"

"I'm still here," Ankhe replied.

"By all the gods, let me out!" Ida cried out. "I'm sorry!"

"Not as sorry as you're going to be," Ankhe promised.

Ida sobbed loudly.

"How dark and tight it must be in there," Ankhe taunted. "How little air."

Ida began screaming uncontrollably, her fierce struggles against her confinement beginning once more with renewed vigor.

Ankhe laughed. She went to her men. "Release her before she suffocates," she instructed.

As one of the men moved towards the coffin, Ankhe held up a hand. "Not just yet. She still has fight in her to spare."

"Yes, my queen," he replied.

With that, the queen left the room, the sounds of Ida's hysterics following her down the corridors of the dark dungeon, bringing laughter to her heart.

XI

Things between Ida and the queen were never the same afterwards. How could they be? Every time Ida saw Tutankh, Ankhe sent her men.

Ida never knew what form her punishment would take.

Sometimes she was locked in a modified confine or a coffin or a box of some sort. Sometimes it was empty. Sometimes it contained water or mud or insects of various varieties.

Always they waited until Pharaoh was away. Always she was released in just enough time to recover sufficiently enough as not to arouse his suspicion.

No matter how careful Ida tried to be, somehow Ankhe always knew.

Ida didn't know if it was Batau, Esnai, someone else or a combination of spies who watched her. It became so she could trust no one.

The only time Ida felt secure and loved

from then onward had been when she was in Tutankh's arms or with Heketya. Even then she could never quite relax between the lies she was forced to tell and the constant fear of being taken.

Still, Tutankh was one of the only two good things in her life, the one person she had that truly belonged to her, one of only two people who truly loved her.

She would never give him up. Even if it killed her.

A couple of months after the split with Queen Ankhesenpaaten, Ankhe had taken Heketya on a trip to Gebtu. Pharaoh Tutankhamun, at that same time, was away on a journey of diplomacy to of all places, Hattusa. Ida had never felt so isolated, so alone.

One day, out of the blue, Gizo had come to her, Galeno just behind him. They carried an order from the queen citing her hosts' slaves as incompetent and ordering Ida to Gebtu.

Ida had never been so afraid in all her life. Though she racked her brain, she could come up with no good reason why she was not able to comply with the queen's command.

Her mind finally numb, she had mechanically gathered her things.

The journey to Ankhe's side had been arduous, wearying. She had fallen asleep.

When she awoke, she found herself near the mouth of a network of caverns.

"Why are we stopping here?" she asked Galeno.

"These are our orders," he said. "You are to go on alone from here. Go though the entrance to that cave and wait." He gestured to it as he spoke.

Ida's eyes followed his hand. As she stared into the forbidding darkness, fear gripped her chest and squeezed.

She grabbed Galeno's arm.

"Is this a trap?" she whispered. "Does she mean to bury me alive?"

"I don't know why she has sent you here," he replied, "or why you would think she means you harm. However, I do know these caves. I used to come here before...to...."

He did not need to finish his sentence. Ida knew well what he meant. It was where he and his male lover met.

In silence, Galeno had dismounted before helping her down, before giving her rations and water.

"I don't know what you have done to incur the queen's ire," Gizo said, "but no matter what happens, we will come back for you as soon as we can."

Ida nodded.

"Now pay attention," Galeno said.

Ida nodded.

She watched as he drew a rough map in the sand with his finger.

"If you get in trouble, don't stop until you find the cavern of the skulls. It is one of the first 6 on the right side. Cross over the skulls and slip into the crevice. Follow the crevice until it gives to two tunnels. Take the left one. Turn right at the 3rd opening. Go down until you find a 2nd crevice. Squeeze into it. It goes on for quite some time but there is a lake at the end of it. There's edible vegetation, some fish."

Ida nodded.

He stood and kissed her temple.

"It grows late," he said. "We must go."

Again, Ida nodded.

Though tears stung at her eyes, Ida steeled herself and took a few steps through the entrance. Then, having no other choice, she sat down and awaited her fate.

Ida was not sure how long she had sat there in that cavern, but during that time, she had emptied both water bags and eaten what little rations the two men were able to spare. She had waited until the little sunlight visible through the gaps and crevices in the rock began to fade.

Ida stood now, began moving groggily towards the entrance.

Voices. Two of Horemheb's spies.

She could not let them find her.

Ida ran.

Searching desperately, she at last spied the skull cavern. She took a deep inhale and squeezed through the crevice.

As Galeno had bade, she followed his instructions until at last the path gave way to the tiny expanse of lake.

Ida collapsed, gasping for air.

Her breath finally returning to normal, she took in her surroundings.

It was truly a little oasis. In addition to the lake and vegetation, there was a wide gap that ran across the massive cavern ceiling. Light streamed in.

Ida heavily made her way to the water's edge. She drank from her cupped hands. She lay on her back and stared up at the sky until she fell asleep.

At first Ida though it a dream.

She had become aware of his scent, then the soft brush of fingers pulling her hair back from her throat. His teeth were gentle on the end of her ear lobe.

A soft smile spread across her lips.

She turned her head and felt the soft press of another mouth against hers, the gently coaxing of a tongue seeking entrance. She welcomed it, rose to press her body against the lean male one that was now on top of her. Her hands tangled in his hair as his hands slid along the length of her body.

The kiss broke and she opened her eyes. She was smiling.

"Do you often allow strange men to

molest you?" Tutankhaten asked her.

She laughed. "How could it be anyone else but you?"

"You peeked?"

She shook her head. "I'd know you anywhere...the smell of you, the feel of your touch, the way you kiss me, the way your body feels against mine."

The slow, half smile that spread across his lips, the gleam in his eyes made her heart pound.

"I'm sorry it took me so long to arrive," he said. "I had meant to be here before you, to surprise you and come with you through the chasm.

"I had it all planned out. I feigned sickness this morning and begged not to be disturbed until tomorrow. I slipped into this peasant dress and made my way out of the citadel easily enough.

"Just as I came over that last rise, I spotted the strangest thing - Horemheb's men just ahead of me."

Ida's mood darkened, her thoughts floating unbidden to the hell she would have to endure when she returned.

He smiled.

"Don't worry," he said. "I was never in any real danger. Even *I* can outsmart those two."

Ida laughed.

He stroked her face. "But if they had found you, had hurt you in any way...."

Ida put two fingers over his lips. "I'm fine," she reassured him.

"But the crevices-" he began.

"I got through the crevice the same way I get through the passageways to your rooms. I closed my eyes and pictured you on the other side."

He grasped the hand at his mouth and kissed her fingers.

"But the passageways are wide," he said. "It must have been hell for you to come here alone."

She softly touched his face. "But it was worth every second to end up here with you."

He sighed. "How I ache when we're apart. I see glimpses of you and I almost go mad with longing."

"Well, we can't let the Pharaoh go mad now can we?" she said as she shifted.

He was hard against her. It heightened

her own excitement.

She slid her hands slowly down his back, then at his waist, around to the front to him.

He whispered her name hoarsely. "Ida."

She grinned sensually, relished the ragged sound of his breath as she touched him. His eyes flashed devilishly then his hand was upon her throbbing womanhood. She gasped and he chuckled deep in his throat.

It was instantaneous. Both of their hands disengaged as if by some instinctive agreement. Hands freed flesh from clothing.

As he thrust into her, her legs wrapped around him. Their mouths battled in frenzied desire.

When they at last exploded in shuddering ecstasy, he had lay his head against her chest. She played with his hair with one hand, the other on his shoulder. His arms were wrapped around her waist.

She could have stayed there with him like that for the rest of her life.

As he drifted into a light slumber, her thoughts turned to Ankhe, to the price she would have to pay for this little snatch of happiness.

Her mind raced, searched desperately for some way to keep this latest rendezvous a secret.

She was so absorbed in her thoughts in fact, that she hadn't even realized he had come awake, that he was studying her intensely.

"What's wrong?" he finally asked.

"Nothing," Ida lied, forcing a smile.

"Ida..."

Ida's gaze fled his. "It's just... I don't want this to end."

Tutankh cupped her cheek. "It won't," he promised. "Ever."

She forced another smile, kissed him deeply.

He broke the kiss, his eyes searching hers. "You *would* tell me if something was wrong, wouldn't you, Ida?"

"Of course I would," she lied. *And have Ankhe turn against you and ally with your enemies?*

"Ankhe hasn't found out has she?" he asked.

"Of course not. No one has. We've been too careful." Yet another lie.

"I know you, Ida. Something is wrong. It's been wrong for a while now."

"*Nothing* is wrong. I just get a little sad sometimes. I miss you."

He shook his head. "You're hiding something."

Ida laughed. "What could I *possibly* be hiding?"

"Ida.."

"Tutankh, please," she begged. "We have so little time together as it is. Let's not do this again. Let's not ruin it by bringing the outside world into it."

He looked away from her.

Ida turned his face back to hers. "I swear it. I'm fine."

"If anyone tries to hurt you, in any way," he said, "even Ankhe, you come to me."

"No one would dare hurt me. I belong to you."

"Promise me, Ida."

"I promise," she lied.

Though he had still seemed suspicious, he had let it drop.

As fate would have it, it would be the last time she would see him alive.

Ida lay now in her bed in the Hittite

citadel. She let out a lonely, pitiful sob, holding herself tightly.

With all of these memories assaulting her like waking dreams, she had to ask herself if it'd all been worth it.

Without a moment's hesitation, the answer came to Ida.

Yes.

Her only true regret was that she hadn't given in to their love sooner, that they hadn't had more time together.

She touched her hand to her softly swollen belly.

Gods, yes. It had definitely been worth it.

She reached inside of her tunic and felt the pin.

XII

The sudden great commotion outside of Ida's rooms in the citadel awoke her. She rose and slid on her dress.

The door to her rooms burst opened. There was a blur of dark silhouettes. Someone grabbed her arms roughly and half dragged her out onto the terrace.

There was an enormous throng below carrying torches and weapons.

"Kill her!" someone yelled.

"Throw her over!" another shouted.

The mob was hungry for her blood.

"But I've done nothing wrong!" Ida exclaimed.

Someone lifted Ida and placed her on the railing as if to throw her to the mob. The mad frenzy below grew.

They were shouting, pushing each other, fighting amongst themselves to get a position closer to the balcony. People were disappearing within the sea of angry Hittites, trampled underfoot.

"Stop this madness, this instant!" a familiar voice boomed from just inside the open terrace doors.

Her assailants turned to face its source.

Mursili.

He and Nacamakun appeared now on the balcony, Mursili's guard surrounding the crowd on the ground below.

"Release the girl," Mursili commanded.

Her assailants looked to one another, confused. They were not accustomed to taking orders from this royal whelp.

"By Telipinu's will, I am your Prince and I order you to release her!"

Ida's assailants relented – with great reluctance.

A path made, Nac made his way to her side. He took her from the oaf that had put her on the railing, setting her feet back down on the ground. He blocked her from the other men's reach with his form.

"But she set the trap for Prince Zannanza," one of the conspirators protested to Mursili.

"She knew not of the plot to kill my brother," Mursili replied. "She has been under my careful surveillance since her arrival and she has conspired with no one.

"Surely you have no doubts as to the competence of a Prince of the Hittites?"

"Of course not, my Prince," the man replied. "Perhaps she came here knowing from the start what they had planned."

Ida pushed passed Nac to face her accusers. "I only came here to save my queen from the evil men who threaten to seize control of Egypt - Ay and Horemheb," she replied impassioned. "It is *they* who have plotted to undo not only Prince Zannanza but my Queen. It is *they* who killed Pharaoh and tried to make it seem an accident. It is *they* who have done all of this and more.

"Prince Mursili is right. I am innocent."

"See, Great Prince?" one of the men replied. "How well the little viper spins her lies, even now."

"It matters not your decision," Mursili said. "Only the King has the power to pass a judgment of death."

He took Ida's arm and hurriedly led her from the room, Nac right behind them.

The men on the terrace protested angrily. Though they followed the three they dared not challenge Nacamakun.

In the corridor, a small command of soldiers came to block their path.

"I am taking her to the king," Mursili said releasing her, one hand on the hilt of his weapon. "Stand aside or die."

The soldiers looked uncertain. While Mursili was 4th Prince, the deceptively thin and fairly introverted teenager was not one from whom they had ever been instructed to take order.

"Now!" Mursili growled as Ida leaned weakly against him.

The soldiers obeyed.

"Carry her," Mursili ordered Nac.

Nacamakun lifted her easily into his arms, hurried behind Mursili towards the throne room. They were well on their way when someone grabbed Ida's arm and pulled her from Nac's grasp. Ida screamed.

Nacamakun turned, pulled her free again before he began to scuffle with the man. More men came to the aide of Ida's assailant.

Mursili grabbed hold of her arm once more, pushed her behind him as he fought beside Nac.

"Ida, run!" Mursili gasped after one man got the better of him, slashing his arm.

Ida did as she was bade. She flew to the throne room and threw open the door.

She ran down its great length towards the hurriedly clad men who clustered around the man on the throne. She fell on her knees before them.

One of the men drew a dagger and raised it to plunge it through the base of her skull. A 2nd dagger flew at him, piercing his arm. The man dropped the knife.

Mursili went to the man and pulled his knife from the man's wrist. He wiped the man's blood on the man's clothes.

Mursili turned now to King Suppiluliuma. "Sire, I bring Idamun here for your judgment and your judgment alone."

"Then have it," Suppiluliuma answered. "For what has happened to my son, she and her kind shall be put to death,"

"But she is with child," Mursili said. "Nacamakun's child."

"Nacamakun's child?" Suppilu repeated. "How can you be sure this girl tells the truth?"

"I learned of it not from her mouth but

from Clizi's."

The King studied Mursili skeptically for a long moment before he turned to Nac.

"Is this true?" he asked.

Nacamakun nodded.   "Yes, sire," he lied. "The child is mine."

The king stood and walked to the window.   He stared out of it as he weighed Mursili's words.

Just what was the witch's son up to? His behavior, when it came to this girl, had been far out of his usual character - to put it mildly. Could the child somehow be Mursili's and Nac, loyal to the boy to a fault, be covering for him?

The King frowned.

Nac would do most anything for Mursili, even something like this.

King Suppilu turned back to them at length.   He looked at Ida who was still prostrate, then to Mursili and the old soldier.

At last he spoke. "Because you have so faithfully served me Nacamakun, I make this edict. No harm is to come to Idamun whilst she is with child.

"She is to serve the court as any other slave might so long as she is able to do so. I will not pass judgment on her until after the baby is let from her body."

"And then?" Mursili asked.

"The child shall stay with Nacamakun."

"And Ida? She is still the child's mother," Mursili pressed. "Surely, it would only be true justice to spare her."

"Justice? You dare speak to me of justice for this creature?!" the King demanded moving menacingly towards Ida.

Mursili quickly moved forward and pulled Ida to her feet, out of the King's reach. He stood now in front of her, Nac just behind her.

"Was it justice that Zannanza, your own brother, was murdered?!" the King demanded.

Mursili knew better than to answer. Any further point he tried to make now would be wrong in his father's eyes.

"A postponement of her sentence is all I am willing to offer you, boy," the King said. "Take it."

Mursili bowed his head. "As you have bidden, My King."

He and Nac waited, heads bowed respectfully as the King and his entourage left the chamber.

"What now, My Prince?" Nac asked.

"He said she is to serve the court did he not?" Mursili asked.

"Indeed."

"Well I'm a member of court am I not?"

"You are," Nac replied.

"And the child is to remain in your care?"

"Yes."

"Then we'll both take her to the house in Syria. She will be safe under my brother Sarri's protection."

"And your father?"

"Let Sarri and I worry about father. You just have our quarters packed and ready to go by first light."

"Yes, sire," the grizzled soldier replied. "But what is to be done with the girl until then?"

"Ida will stay with me in my rooms until the household is ready to move."

"Yes, sire."

Mursili waited until Nac left the throne room before he grabbed Ida's wrist and triggering a hidden door, led her through the passageways to his quarters.

Ida was lost in speculation. She stood

there, unseeingly, as Mursili gave his guard instruction and barricaded his chamber door.

He turned now to look at the girl. "You can share the bed," he said.

Ida looked over at him. "Why are you doing this?" she asked.

"If you think I mean to take advantage - "

"I mean why are you helping me?"

"Why not?" he replied flippantly. "I'm a Prince. You're a pregnant woman. What kind of a man would stand by and watch a pregnant woman be murdered?"

"Man? You're still a boy."

"Perhaps, but a boy who is man enough to protect you."

"And to go against your father?"

"It's about time someone did," he replied. "And who better than the witch's son?"

He rolled up his sleeve, examined the wound on his arm.

"The witch's son?"

"The old gypsy woman at the banquet who cornered you."

"The fortune teller?" Ida asked.

"She's my mother, my exiled mother."

Suddenly it all made sense to Ida. "So you believe it too. You believe that this child I carry is somehow destined to save the Amarna line."

"I believe what the gods have shown me," Mursili replied.

"And just what is that?"

"That your fate and my fate, that the fate of the Hittites and the fate of the Amarnas are intertwined. If one falls, they both fall. If one rises, they both will rise."

Ida laughed humorlessly.

"What's so funny?" he asked as he applied salve to his cut.

"That you people think I or any child issuing from me is special. That you think I have the strength to guide and protect this child, that I have it in me to fight against your father, Ay and Horemheb."

"It doesn't matter to me if you believe. It only matters that you and your line survives. Nac and I are going to make sure that that happens."

"And just how are you going to do that?" Ida demanded. "Do you even realize how many times tonight alone my child and I were almost killed?"

"I know exactly how many times you

were almost killed tonight. Nacamakun and I were there, remember? And we kept the both of you safe, didn't we?"

"Maybe you got lucky. Maybe we all did. But how much longer do you think you can possibly delay the inevitable?"

Mursili shrugged. "I think you'd be surprised."

"Don't kid yourself," Ida replied. "I knew my life would be a short one the moment I gave in to my feelings for Pharaoh, especially after my queen found out. I knew it would be shorter still when he was murdered. Shorter still when I crossed the desert into Hattusa, when I found out I carry Pharaoh's child.

"Now Prince Zannanza's murder has cut my time down to what? Maybe another few months at best?

"You may by some miracle be able to save my child, but don't fool yourself. Be it by Egyptian or Hittite hands, I will not live to see 20."

"Maybe you will," Mursili countered. "Maybe you won't. That still doesn't mean I will ever give up fighting for you."

Ida laughed harshly.

"What's the point, Mursili?!" she asked.

"To fulfill some outlandish prophecy? I can't even leave this *room* by myself."

Her laughter turned to hysterical sobs. "Even if I do make it out of Hattusa alive, I will have to spend the rest of my life in hiding from one faction or the other."

"A life in hiding is better than no life at all," he replied.

He stared at her for a long moment.

"Don't you think you've wasted enough time and energy on self-pity?" he asked.

Ida was taken aback, momentarily forgetting her despair.

"What?!" she choked.

"I have no plans to spend the next months listening to you cry every time the wind blows. It certainly can't be good for your baby either."

He nodded. "I know now why your queen sent you here. She was sick of your whining, wasn't she?"

Ida's tears were all but forgotten in her temper.

"How dare you?" she demanded. "You think my life has been easy? You think these tears have been easy?

"I have just lost everything I ever cared about. *Everything.* And you dare mock my pain?"

She shook her head. "I would rather take my chances in my own rooms in the citadel than be trapped in Syria for a *hundred years* with a spoiled jackass like you."

She stormed towards the door.

Mursili smiled, applauding.

Ida whirled around to face him.

"Good for you," he said. "You do still have a backbone after all."

"You don't know a damned thing about me," Ida spat.

"I know that you're a lot tougher than you let on. I know that there is a great deal of fire and resiliency behind that puffy, weepy face of yours."

He moved towards her. "I know that you carry the child of Pharaoh Tutankhamun - whom you obviously loved a great deal and who loved you enough to claim you to wife. I know you faked your own death and snuck here right under the nose of the very same men that just a few minutes ago you claimed you could not outmaneuver. I know when you thought that mob on the terrace might turn on me, you risked yourself to try to make them understand the truth.

"I also know you're right about me. Many would call me an ass.

"While my advice is sound, it is often delivered with far too much pragmaticism to be palatable to even the slightly sentimental. However, I am good at keeping confidences and most all would agree that there is no one better to have on your side or more loyal than I.

"I'm also not tactful like my older brothers or as war-worn as my father, but I'm learning."

He gave a small smile. "You should also keep in mind that asses are stubborn. Asses don't give up - no matter what."

Ida stood uncertainly at the door.

"Give it a try," he said. "What's the worst that could happen if you cast your lot with me?"

"I could end up dead," Ida replied.

Mursili laughed. "You'll probably end up dead either way, just that much sooner if you try to go it on your own."

A soft chuckle escaped Ida's lips inspite of herself.

"Now what say you help me bandage this

arm?" he asked.

When she continued to stand there uncertainly, he added. "Don't worry. You'll have plenty of time to run away later."

Ida hesitated for another long moment. Then, with little other choice, she went to him and began to dress his wound.

XIII

Time is man's greatest enemy. No one knew this better than Idaten. The last year and a half had simply flown by.

Though Ida had a determined and resourceful ally in Prince Mursili, she knew well that each day she spent in the Syrian palace was borrowed. It was only a matter of time before the chaos that had broken out in the wake of Prince Zannanza's death seeped through the cracks of even these high stone walls.

Every morning she woke with a mixture of relief and dread. Every night she went to sleep with a mixture of hope and fear.

In spite of the happiness of her days there, there was always this anxiety gnawing at her. It was worse than waiting for Ankhe's guards to find her and lock her in the confines.

Some days she almost wished it would all collapse already, that this half nightmare, half dream would end.

Adding to Ida's unease, Mursili had

been summoned to the capital, his father having fallen victim to the plague. He had been gone for almost a month now, each day of his absence adding to Ida's dread.

As Ida watched her son stumble clumsily about the yard, laughing merrily as he chased Nacamakun's 3-year-old son, Kadar, she wished it would never end.

Her son, Abidos, was so beautiful. He looked more like her than Tutankh - which she was certain might well save his life one day. He possessed Tutankh's gentle nature, though sparks of Ida's fire showed through when he was angry.

Abidos fell on top of Kadar, laughing so hard tears filled his eyes. He didn't even seem to mind Kadar's flailing, as the other boy struggled to slip from his grasp.

Kadar's mother had given birth to him 2 months too early and had died shortly thereafter. It was a miracle that the little boy himself had survived. He was very small for his age and prone to fits of illness. Her son dwarfed him.

Abidos clumsily climbed to his feet and began to run after the little boy who had finally managed to escape him. Again, Abidos fell.

Ida chuckled softly.

She was so absorbed in the little boys' play, in fact, that she did not even hear Clizi come out.

"Ida," Clizi called softly from behind her.

Ida turned to look at her.

"Prince Mursili has returned," the old woman said.

"Is he in his rooms?" Ida asked rising.

Clizi nodded. Ida did not fail to notice that the old woman would not look her in the eye.

Stiffly, Ida made her way to Mursili's rooms. She hesitated outside of the door for a time, gathering her composure.

When finally she entered, she found Mursili pacing frantically. He stopped suddenly, picked up a statuette and flung it violently against the wall.

Ida gasped.

He turned to face her.

"Ida," he breathed.

"Are you alright?" she asked quietly.

Mursili shook his head. "I warned him, Ida," he said, his anguish etched upon his handsome features. "I warned him of the folly of attacking Egypt without first consulting the oracle and receiving the gods' blessings. I warned him about gloating over his ill-won victory and bringing the Egyptian captives to Hattusa.

"Even the *gods* tried to warn him, Ida. They brought forth first a plague upon our people. When he heeded them not, the drought came.

"Even with all of this, arrogant, foolish King Suppiluliuma, breaker of the covenant of the Telepenus's Proclamation, refused to heed.

"Now he lies dead - a victim of the very plague he carried here from Egypt."

Tears pooled in his eyes.

"Oh, Mursili," Ida breathed. "I'm so sorry."

"The old fool brought it upon himself," he said sitting down heavily upon the stair, his head hanging down.

Ida went to him. She sat down beside him, intertwining her hands with his. They sat there in silence for a long while.

"Prince Arnuwanda's coronation is imminent," he said quietly.

He needn't say more.

Ida knew well what it meant. Prince Arnuwanda and his wife Mal-Nikal had made no secret of their desire to execute all Egyptians within their borders, a sacrifice to the gods in hopes of regaining their favor. They had been Mursili's greatest enemies when it came to Ida. Now, with Suppilu out of the way, they would come for her.

"I'm sorry," he continued, "but there's nothing more I can do. I can no longer keep you safe here."

Ida nodded, silent tears falling from her eyes.

"I got to see 20 at least," she said.

They both chuckled softly.

She sobered.

"How long do I have?" she asked.

Mursili's smile faded.

He rose, went to stare out of one of his windows. "You leave tomorrow."

"I see," she replied, she too rising.

Mursili turned back to face her.

"I'd better go spend time with my son," she said wiping away her tears and struggling to regain her composure.

She turned to leave.

"Ida," Mursili began, walking towards her.

She turned back to face him.

"In time," he said, "when things blow over..."

"I know," she replied.

She then did something she had wanted to do for many months now. She placed a lingering kiss upon his lips.

Mursili was taken aback but for a moment before he pulled her to him and kissed her back.

A noise in the antechamber broke them apart.

As Ida turned to go, Mursili grabbed her hand. He held it for a long moment before letting it go.

Ida lay awake in her bed late that night, Abidos asleep on her chest as she stroked his back.

She could not bear to think of leaving her son, would not allow herself to until she was well away from him - knowing now that losing him would be the blow that killed her.

Still, there was no scenario she could

image in which Abidos would be safer with her than with Mursili and Nac. Once she crossed that border into Egypt, it was only a matter of time before her enemies found her. She would not let them destroy Abidos too.

The child began to fuss in his sleep, interrupting the train of her thoughts.

Ida rose, began to pace the room as she gently bounced the boy in her arms, as she soothingly stroked his face.

Her thoughts turned to Mursili.

Mursili was no longer the quiet, lanky boy he had been when first they had met. Their time in Syria and the challenge of protecting her had strengthened his body as well as his mind.

The two of them had grown close these months. Very close. So close, in fact, that she felt guilty - as if she were betraying Tutankh somehow by having feelings for this man. Still, Ida could not see how she could not care for Mursili.

Mursili had taken good care of them, had been with her every step of the way. He had never let her feel sorry for herself, always coming up with some distraction or goading her into an argument or project until the dark thoughts were driven away.

He had shown her her first snow, held her hand when she went into labor. He had been the first man to hold Abidos and remained to this day Abidos' favorite person outside of Ida. He had held her when she cried, listened tirelessly as she rambled on and on about her dead Pharaoh and all she had suffered under Ankhe.

He was the first person in her life, the only person she had never lied to, that she had never pretended with. She felt free with him, like it was safe for her to be Ida in spite of all of the baggage that came with it.

Could she now just give that up and go back to the way she was? Back to all the lies and the paranoia and isolation?

After all they had been through, could she really just leave him now, now when his world was on the verge of falling apart?

Though she did not, could not love him in quite the same way she had loved Tutankh, she had to admit to herself now, before it was too late, that her feelings for him were no less real. Mursili was under her skin.

Ida's mind drifted to their earlier

encounter in his chamber.

After tomorrow, she may well never see him again.

If Arnuwanda's forces had their way, she was dead. If Ay, Horemheb or Ankhe caught her, she was also dead. And that was only *if* the perils of the journey, her broken heart or slavers didn't remove her from the equation first.

Setting Abidos in his bed, Ida kissed his forehead. She stared down at him for another long moment before leaving the room.

Ida found Mursili awake. He was staring, unseeingly, out of the window. He turned to glance briefly in her direction as she entered, before returning his gaze to the sky.

Ida's heart pounded loudly in her ears as she shut the door and moved towards him.

Though he did not turn, Mursili was acutely aware of her approach. His chest heaved, his blood rushing loudly in his ears. The task of not turning towards her was becoming more and more unbearable with each passing second.

She was right behind him now. He could feel her there though she had yet to speak or touch him.

Behind him, Ida reached out a hand to touch his arm, pulled it back before it made contact. She stood there uncertainly for what felt like an eternity, her resolve fast abandoning her.

And there he was, his back to her, pretending she wasn't even there.

Maybe this was a mistake, Ida thought. Maybe he didn't feel the same way about her. Maybe Mursili was being the gentleman he was, trying to make an already ridiculous situation less so.

She turned to go instead, was surprised when Mursili grabbed her by her wrist, holding her fast. She looked up into his eyes. They glittered like jewels in the torchlight.

His mouth came down hard upon hers, the long-denied desire consuming them both without thought, without care for what was to come.

He gently guided her backward towards the bed, hands leisurely divesting bodies of clothing and mouths rarely losing connection.

He carefully laid her naked form down

upon the bed, covered her body with his.

He stared now into her eyes, said a million things in that silence that neither of them dared give voice to before he reclaimed her mouth.

The rest of the night slipped away unnoticed as they explored each other's bodies, as he forever removed any doubts from her mind that Mursili was no longer a boy but a man.

Dawn broke far too soon.

The household would be awake any time now. She could linger no longer.

Silently, they kissed their goodbyes. Then Ida quietly padded back to her rooms.

XIV

The next day went all too quickly for Ida. By late afternoon, her escort was preparing to start out.

Ida was playing with Abidos in their rooms when Nacamakun came to her.

"Ida," he began.

"I know," she replied, though she hesitated.

Tears pooled in her eyes, a thousand conflicting thoughts and emotions flowing through her all at once.

She took a deep, shaky breath before at last picking up Abidos. She held him to her, stroking his hair.

As she turned to face Nac, she spoke. "I know I have already asked too much of you, of all of you, but I'm *begging* you. Please take my son as your own."

"I promise you," he replied. "So long as I have breath in me, no harm shall come to him. Everything Kadar will have so will Abidos.

"And I won't be alone either. No

grandmother could love him more than Clizi and no father could fight harder for him than Prince Mursili."

Ida nodded, the tears falling.

She reached into her shift and took off the pin Tutankh had given her. "Give this to him when he begins to become a man. Never let him doubt that I loved him more than my own breath, that he was conceived in purest love between a man and a woman."

Nacamakun took it from her, looked down at it.

He looked back up at her. In that moment, Ida knew he knew well what it was.

"You have my word," he promised.

Ida nodded again.

When she continued to stand fast he spoke again. "It's time."

Though Ida nodded, her grip on Abidos tightened.

"Ida..."

She at last forced her legs to carry her out of the room and into the courtyard.

The caravan was ready. Clizi and others were gathered to say their goodbyes.

Mursili was not among them.

Ida barely heard anything any of them said to her, bore their kisses and hugs stiffly as she slowly made her way towards the caravan.

She stood just short of her horse, frozen, Abidos still in her arms.

"Ida," Nac urged. "He will never be safe in Egypt, never as your son."

"I know," she replied.

When she continued to stand frozen, Clizi approached. "I'll take him," she said softly, reaching out her arms for the boy.

Ida looked to the old woman, the pity in Clizi's eyes almost unbearable. She began to tremble. She turned her back to her.

"Mommy loves you so much," Ida said to Abidos. "Always. Always. Always. More than all the treasures in the world. More than the sun, the moon and the stars. Never forget that." She planted a lingering kiss on his head.

She turned now to Clizi, gave the boy over to her.

"I'm sorry, Ida," the old woman said before hurriedly carrying the boy away.

As if sensing something was wrong, very wrong, Abidos began to cry and squirm in Clizi's arms. He cried out for his mother. Over and over again he cried out, his cries ripping into Ida's very soul.

It would be the first time in his life that his mother would not come.

Ida no longer had the strength to stand. She sank to the ground, stared through tear blurred eyes in the direction in which Clizi had carried her son.

Nac watched her uneasily. He was no good at this sort of thing. Where the hell was Mursili?!

Almost as if hearing Nac's thoughts, Mursili appeared. He stared at her for a long moment before he sank down to his knees before her.

"Ida," he said softly.

Slowly, she turned her gaze to his.

The sorrow in his eyes was too much. A great, heaving sob shook Ida. He pulled her into his arms, held her tightly. More heart wrenching sobs came, the flood of her grief finally spilling forth. In all his life, Mursili would never forget how she had cried.

He let her feel sorry for herself but for a few moments before he pulled away. He held her now, firmly by her shoulders.

"I need you to listen to me," he said, his

eyes boring into hers. "I know this is hard, the hardest thing you have had to endure yet, but you need to be strong right now. We *all* need you to be strong, but most especially Abidos needs you to. The longer you linger, the more danger you put us all in."

Ida stared at him for a long moment. Then, with more strength than even she knew she had, Ida began to fight her grief, to bring her sorrow back under control.

"Good girl," he said. "I won't let them win. Things *will* get better. I promise you. And, when they do, you can return.

"But if Arnu or his queen or many others like them get their hands on you, it's all over. *Everything* is over.

"You need to leave *now*, before it's too late. You have to be gone before Arnu's coronation, before his proclamations become public knowledge."

Ida took a deep breath, shaky breath. She pulled away from him and stood. Mursili rose as well.

Silently, he helped her mount her horse, watched as she struggled valiantly not to fall apart. He took her hand in his, pressed it to his lips. Ida turned to look at him, their gazes holding for a long moment before he released her hand and backed away.

The caravan lurched forward.

"If any harm comes to her," Mursili proclaimed, "there will be nowhere for the man who lets her be hurt to hide."

"Sire," his men intoned.

He stood back helplessly, watching them go.

XV

Egypt. Ida had never loathed any place as much as she did her beloved Egypt at this moment.

As they neared the border, she could see it was still just as beautiful as it had always been.

Still, in her heart, it no longer felt like home - not without Abidos, not without Tutankh. She was certainly no longer the same girl who had slipped across the border almost 2 years ago.

She gazed out now at the riverbank, saw she, Tutankh and Ankhe playing there when they were children.

It seemed so long ago.

A couple of miles across the Egyptian border, the caravan came to a halt. The head of the caravan and Nac spoke briefly, after which the caravan veered southeast, leaving Ida and her escort behind.

Ida's escort led her through Lower Egypt.

It was only when they continued on around Thebes that Ida became confused.

She rode up alongside Nac.

"Where are you taking me?" she asked him.

"Upper Egypt."

"Upper Egypt?" she asked, her confusion growing.

"Napata."

"Napata?! I know no one in Napata."

"Good," Nac replied. "We were not certain."

"But why?"

"Prince Mursili asked that I make sure you arrive safely and that's what I intend to do."

"In Thebes. But Napata?"

"The Prince has a great many allies, even in Upper Egypt. We have only a fraction of an idea of what Arnuwanda's next move will be, of his agenda as a whole. Mursili does not want you anywhere near the northern border."

"And I am to survive how in Napata?"

"The Prince has secured you a position with a noble family there....as a wet nurse."

"A what?!" she asked. She felt as if the wind had been knocked out of her.

"You can trust in Mursili, Ida. His plans have plans have plans."

"A wet nurse?!" she breathed shaking her head. "How could he?"

"He cares a great deal for you, Ida. Even so, he knew well the day would come when you would have to return home."

"So he forces me away to strangers, to a land I've never been to, into a trade that he of all people should know I could not do?" she asked.

"Sometimes, we all have to do things we wish we did not."

Ida fell silent for a long moment. "And how can you even be sure we can trust these people?"

"As Mursili is sure, so am I," he replied. "But then Mursili's plans have plans have plans. Should you need it, you will find more than enough in your packs for any eventuality.

"Still, money can only get you so far. People you can truly trust are hard to come by in these turbulent times."

Ida fell into silence as she contemplated Napata and her alternatives. There was little of appeal to choose from in any scenario.

"Will they know who I am?" she asked

at length.

Nac remained impassive. "The household only know what they need to know. Your husband was killed in the Hittite Sac. Your daughter died in a cart accident shortly thereafter. You have served in two prominent households in wet nurse capacity and come highly recommended."

"And if I refuse this post?"

"Then I shall have no choice but to remain by your side."

Ida scoffed.

"The Prince has determined that you will live to a ripe old age," Nac added, "that you will return to him."

"And the children?" Ida asked. "Mursili? Who will protect them while you're here babysitting me?"

"I trust my men."

"Your men?"

"Prince Mursili and his household were ordered back to the citadel. He in turn ordered the boys be taken to my private estate in Hattusa - out of Arnuwanda's sight but close enough should he need to act."

"So I have even less choice than even I

knew?" Ida asked.

"In Napata you will have comfort, protection, an open conduit to the Prince should you need it and a legitimate reason to keep your milk flowing – a thing that might be useful should you be able to return before Abidos reaches his 3rd year."

Ida studied Nac's face for a long moment. "Alright," she conceded. "I will do as Mursili wishes."

XVI

Will I ever get used to it? Ida wondered as she sat at the mirror and brushed her long, blonde locks.

It had been nearly 2 years since she had come to Napata and still she saw a golden-haired stranger whenever she looked in the mirror.

It had been Lord Bietek's mandate that she dye her hair, as it had been that she take on the name Hawara.

She set down the brush, absently stroked her wrist where her bracelet had been. Upon Nac's instance she had given it over to him for safekeeping – it so obviously being a token of imperial favor.

She began to braid her hair.

Yes, it had been yet another lifetime since she had arrived - the Bietek edifice almost as impressively defensible as Mursili's estate in Syria. Lord Bietek, a staunch supporter of the Amarna line and of peace between the Hittites

& Egypt, had proven stern but trustworthy.

It had been difficult at first for her to mask her broken heart, to touch, let alone to hold and suckle someone else's child.

Still, even that had grown easier.

Ida rose and went to the nursery, knowing well the little Lord would be awake soon. She greeted the other staff as she went.

Inside the nursery, she closed the door, sat down on the window seat as she waited.

Things were not well in the land of the Hittites. Though the drought had finally ended, the plague pressed onward.

King Arnuwanda had been furious to learn that he had been outsmarted by Prince Mursili. Though Prince Sarri made sure no harm came to Mursili, much of Mursili's household was executed. The gods be thanked, Nacamakun and Clizi were not among them.

Mursili had also taken a wife. One who, by all accounts, he had grown to love a great deal. A woman by the name of Gassulawiya.

Still, he had never forgotten Ida. Even to this day, he worked tirelessly on her behalf.

Almost a year ago, Arnuwanda succumbed to the plague leaving his conniving viper of a queen, Mal-Nikal, to rule as

Tawannanna – Queen Dowager and conduit to the gods.

To their vassals' surprise, Mursili had managed somehow to maneuver himself into the position of King. It had outraged many that they should be forced to accept what they considered the inexperienced rule of a man-child - especially when there were two older, seemingly more capable Princes who should have by all right superseded him.

His right to rule was under constant challenge from all sides – from within by Mal-Nikal and her allies, and without by numerous tribes including the Kaskas, the Arzawa and the Kaskans.

In Egypt, Ay and Horemheb still reigned supreme, watched with interest the disorder in the Empire to the North.

They worked steadily to erase all memory of Tutankhamun and his father, Akhenaten, from official record, to undo all that both men had accomplished. Both names were stricken from all public and palatial inscriptions, Ay and Horemheb even going so far as to usurp their monuments.

As of late, rumor had begun to spread

that Ay even intended to steal Tutankhamun's tomb.

It had been almost a month since Lord Bietek had last held private audience with Ida, and now her nerves were on edge. She simply had to know what was going on back in Hattusa, that Abidos, Kadar, Nac & Mursili were still safe.

As it was now, all she could do was pray to the gods and make sacrifices each holy day.

The little Lord cried out, breaking Ida's train of thought. She rose and went to him, soothingly stroking his hair as he began to suckle her.

Lord Bietek's audience chamber was overflowing. Though Ida could find no legitimate reason to be near its doors, she could not stop herself from drawing near.

"How can we be sure it is so?" Lord Bietek demanded.

"How can it not be?" one of the men replied. "Manapa-Tarhunta has betrayed King Mursili. The king and his comrades were ambushed near the Seha River."

"But there were survivors."

"Mostly foot soldiers. Of the commanders only Chief Urhib was found and even he is in and out of lucidity.

"There has been no sign of the King nor the captain of his personal guard, Nacamakun."

Ida could hear no more though the debate continued inside. She stood rooted in shock as tears began to fall from her eyes.

If Mursili had fallen and Nacamakun had fallen ...

Ida could not even bear to think on it.

She suddenly found it difficult to breathe. She had to get out of here, away from this place.

Hurrying to her rooms, Ida began to pack, her vision blurred by her tears.

Home. She needed to go home. She needed to tell Tutankh goodbye, then she needed to go back to the land of the Hittites, to find her son before it was too late.

XVII

When at last Ida came to the Imperial City, she was unrecognizable. Between her Bedouin dress, her blonde locks and her carriage, no one would ever take her for the girl she had once been.

As she moved through the city towards the palace, she was keenly aware of her surroundings.

Once at the palace, she took the hidden corridor to Tutankh's quarters, a corridor she had used a thousand nights before. She wanted something of his she could carry with her, needed to know where he was buried.

At the trap door she listened. Hearing nothing, she slowly pushed it open.

She peered into the chamber. Empty.

She climbed into the room, leaving the door ajar should she need to exit the rooms in a hurry.

She went to his bedroom and began to dig through his things.

She was rummaging now through a

trunk in Tutankhamun's chamber when she came across it - the document which confirmed the rumors about Ay's plans for Tutankh's tomb.

According to the document, everything had already been set into motion to move Tutankh from his rightful place in the Valley of the Kings and to dispose of him. The precious goods in Tutankh's tomb would then be re-inscribed for Ay and when the time came, Ay would be placed in the tomb along side them.

The move would take place in three months time, while the capital was distracted by the Nile Flood Feast.

Ida's mind reeled.

How could even Ay stoop so low?

She shook her head. She would never let that happen. She would never let Ay damn the man she loved for all eternity. She would see Galeno before she left for Hattusa, would make sure that her people beat Ay to Tutankh's tomb.

Folding the document, she slid it into a hidden pocket of her dress. She resumed her dig.

She froze, listened. Yes, someone was

coming.

She hurried back to the trap door. She could hear the voices more clearly now. Someone was definitely in the hidden passageway. Horemheb.

Carefully Ida re-closed the trap door. The last thing she needed was for one of them to find it open and decide to investigate.

Her mind raced. *What now?*

Hoping against hope, she went through the rooms, towards the second hidden passageway in his personal audience chamber. Just as she was about to enter the audience chamber, the main door of the chamber swung open.

Ida hurriedly slid out of sight. She listened.

Ankhe & Ay.

Out of time, Ida managed to scurry back into the connecting room before she was seen.

What was she going to do? She was trapped!

Quietly, Ida padded back into the bed chamber. She pressed her ear to the initial trap door. Silence.

She slowly pulled the door open, carefully maneuvered her torso inside to look around.

Horemheb and his men were still about, no doubt spying on Ankhe & Ay. Stealthily pulling herself back into the bed chamber, she re-closed the door once more.

There was movement to her left. Ay and Ankhe were moving through the rooms.

Ida desperately scanned the bed chamber. Though her eyes landed upon the bed, she stood rooted, the sweat already breaking out all over her body.

They were just outside now.

Without further hesitation, Ida triggered the panel hidden in the bed's base, slid into the cramped compartment before triggering the door closed again.

It was not long before she felt them settle on the bed above her, before she could hear the old man's raspy moans, Ankhe's soft sighs.

Seconds seemed like minutes, minutes like hours as Ida's own psyche turned against her.

Though it had been years, her experiences in the confines had not lost their potency.

Still, she had to endure. She had to do it for Abidos and in some ways she owned it to Mursili & Nac who had sacrificed so much for her survival. She couldn't let it all end - not here and not now.

She clasped a hand over her mouth to stop herself from screaming like a mad woman.

It was only when Ida heard the snores that she dared open the compartment.

She lay there for a long moment, silently gasping for air as the warm air generated in the compartment began to dissipate.

As quietly as she could, Ida crawled towards the door. She had made it all the way to the threshold when she heard the cry.

Scrambling to her feet, she ran desperately through the rooms towards the audience chamber's trap door. She glanced behind her at the scream's source.

Seeing her face, Ankhesenamun screamed again.

Ankhe had just seen a ghost. She hurriedly covered herself as Ay sprang from the bed, still relatively spry for a man of his advanced years.

"Guards!" he bellowed as he gave chase.

Ida pulled open the trap door, was just

about to fly through it when the guard burst into the room and seized her. They held her fast as Ay then Ankhe entered the room.

Ay's jaw dropped as the realization of the spy's identity hit him.

"Take her to a cell," he ordered, "and send for Horemheb."

Ankhesenpaaten hurried back to the bed chamber. She hastily began to dress – even as the guards led Ida from their rooms.

"I have not given you leave," Ay said, entering the bed chamber.

"I am still queen...if only to further your ambition," Ankhesenpaaten said. "Idamun is *my* property. I mean to find out where she's been all this time."

"As do I," Ay replied, the threat clear in both his tone and expression. "As do I."

Ankhe steadily met Ay's glare for a long moment - before she hurried from the room to the dungeons.

"Guards, open the door," Queen Ankhesenamun snapped.

"Pharaoh has instructed us to await

Horemheb," one of the guards replied. "Until then, no one may question the prisoner."

"You dare disobey your Queen?! Idamun is *my* property not my husband's. I have full rights to her."

The guard captain eyed her thoughtfully for a long moment.

"I'll handle this," he stated, dismissing his men. He waited until they were out of view before he extended his hand, expectant.

"What is this?" Ankhe demanded, indignant.

"You know well what it is, Your Highness," the man replied.

Ankhesenamun offered him the only thing of value she had on her at that time – a necklace given to her by Ay. She would see to it that this rapscallion and his hand were parted soon enough.

The man took the proffered bribe with a slimy smirk. He studied it for a long moment. Then, seemingly satisfied, he unlocked the cell.

Ankhesenamun entered.

"I see you haven't lost the common touch," Ida said, not even bothering to look up at her.

Ankhe's blood boiled. "How dare you

come back here," she growled.

"It had to be a surprise to say the least - my return," Ida replied. "With what happened with Zannanza, surely you expected they'd kill me.

"Yet, here I am, alive and blonde."

Ankhe grabbed her up by her hair. "Perhaps your stay in Hattusa has made you forget yourself, but Ida, you are still my property."

Ida pushed her away, her eyes glittering with hatred. "Not anymore, Ankhe. I belong to me now.

"I will; however, honor the vow I made to you all those years ago, to serve you and protect you. Though you have gravely wronged me and dishonored Tutankh, though I despise you and everything you stand for with everything in me, I will not tell anyone of your involvement in this."

"By all the gods you won't," Ankhe threatened.

The door behind them opened. Ankhe turned to face the intruder.

Horemheb.

Horemheb's eyes glittered intensely.

He smiled harshly, his graze drifting from Ankhe to Ida.

"Well, isn't this interesting?" he mused.

He reached out his hand and took a tendril of Ida's hair between his fingers.

"You look very vibrant for a dead woman, Ida." He said to her. "And very wheat-haired."

Ida did not respond.

His gaze returned to Ankhesenpaaten. "And to find you here too, Queen Ankhesenamun.

"This night is just full of surprises, isn't it?"

"She is my property," Ankhe replied. "I have every right to be here."

"To learn as I learn?" Horemheb asked. "Or perhaps to make sure her tongue stays silent against you?"

"She is just a slave. What could she possibly have to say that would be truth in regards to the Queen of all Egypt."

"You'd be surprised what the lowly know, what they are capable of discovering.

"I myself am not from nobility, but have I not .... advised, been that little voice in the heads of three separate god-kings?

"Idamun is a slave, yes. But I'm willing to wager she knows quite a lot."

Ankhesenpaaten fell silent.

"So, Idamun," he said, "Tell me. Where have you been all these years?"

Ida stared at him defiantly.

He sighed exaggeratedly.

"Oh, Ida," he said. "It would be such a shame to ruin such a pretty face."

He reached out and touched her cheek.

Ida pulled away as though he had seared her.

Horemheb chuckled. "I am quite certain I already know the answer to my little question. I mean, how *else* could the Hittites have known so quickly of Tutankhamun's little...accident?"

Ida slapped him.

Horemheb laughed. "I do so admire your fire, girl, your courage. I only wonder how it is that a lamb like Tutankh was able to tame a lioness such as you. I mean aside from the wealth and the power."

Ida did not answer.

"How did you do it, Idamun? Fake your own death?

"Who helped you, *tried* to help you commit treason against Pharaoh?"

Ida laughed harshly now.

"Ah, so now you are amused," Horemheb said.

"I am. I conspired to commit treason against *Pharaoh*? And by Pharaoh, I believe you mean Ay?"

Horemheb smirked, his anger thinly veiled.

Ida continued. "I must admit, I am surprised to have returned to find Ay and not you upon the throne. See as you do so prize yourself of your cunning, deviousness, treachery. How is it that the old turtle beat you to the finish line? How is it that that old man made a fool out of you?"

Horemheb forced a hard smile. "I suppose that even the most unlikely of candidates can worm their way to power - just as a slave girl can worm her way into a god-king's bed.

"But don't fret, Ida. Ay is old and without blood heirs. Accidents happen all the time.

"Surely you know that by now?

"And me... I am a patient man."

"I'm sure Nakhtmin will beg to differ," Ankhe taunted. "Ay means for him to rule in his stead."

Horemheb turned, eyed the queen pointedly. "Surely even you are clever enough to see that your little love toy is hardly a match for me.

"Even if he were, by some miracle, to get within a 100 yards of the throne, how long do you think you'll hold onto him – especially once he finds out about your shriveled, little womb?"

The look of outrage and shock upon Ankhesenamun's face brought a chuckle to Horemheb's throat.

"Yes, I am aware of your plight," Horemheb said with feigned consideration, "but poor ancient Ay, he has no idea that when he dies, his line dies.

"Still, it is a kindness you do the man. Riding a woman as ancient as his wife, Tiy, must be like plowing through the desert with a 50 sna pack."

"No," he mused, a lecherous smile upon his face, "not nearly as desirable as a nice, warm, firm little piece of ass like you, Great

Queen.

"Of course, from your end it must be like getting rutted by a dried out piece of driftwood. Still, we all make sacrifices in the end. Don't we?

"You just keep right on spreading your favor and believing in Ay & Nakhtmin, keep hoping that they can save you from me.

"As for me, I control the military and I dear Ankhesenamun have no room in my court nor in my bed for vipers."

The color drained from the Queen's face.

"You may take your leave now, my Queen," Horemheb suggested.

Ankhesenpaaten stood rooted.

"Now!" he barked.

Ankhe scurried from the room.

Horemheb returned to Ida. He closed the space between them, cornering her.

"There is no need for games," he said. "We both know where you were, why you were there and who sent you there. That quite frankly is a waste of my time," he said waving it away.

"I know you are bound by your oath not to expose your queen, and that you will not -

though you murder her with every glance. You have honor, know the meaning of loyalty though your mistress does not.

"Your little deception is of no real consequence to me. You were only doing as you were commanded, as all good subservients should.

"Besides, I don't need your testimony to condemn Ankhesenamun. The walls are closing in on her, even as we speak."

He grabbed Ida's wrists forcing her hands behind her back. He pressed himself against her.

Ida's eyes glittered angrily.

"I don't want to have to hurt you," he said, "but make no mistake, I will."

He greedily tasted her throat.

Ida's chest heaved with angry outrage.

He abandoned her throat and returned his eyes to her face. "All you have to do is become one of my concubines, swear an oath of allegiance to me."

"Never," she spat.

Fury burned in Horemheb's eyes. "Women all across Egypt would pluck out their own mother's eyes to be a consort of the

Pharaoh, yet you reject me for the love of a dead boy?!"

"Did you forget, Horemheb?" Ida spat. "You are not Pharaoh."

"I am not Pharaoh in title only, and very soon, that too will be remedied."

"Let go of me," Ida demanded.

Horemheb's eyes glittered. "You want me to let go of you?

"As you wish.

"Perhaps you prefer instead to lie with the rats, the rot, the cold, the darkness, the stale bread and water, the disease?"

She did not answer though defiance burned steadily in her eyes.

He released her. "Hykis!" The man appeared at the door. "Lock her in one of the confines."

Horror flashed briefly in Ida's eyes. The confines were only 6 feet by 3 feet, no windows, no air.

Horemheb smiled slowly, then he left Hykis to his charge.

XVIII

Ida was on the verge of insanity three days later. She had clawed at the metal until her nails broke and bled. She had screamed until her voice had failed her. She had balled up as best as she could and wished for dead.

At last her mind fled, a jumble of memories assaulting her all at once - in bits and pieces.

At last exhausted, sleep claimed her.

Ida's peace, however, was short-lived. She was awakened, not an hour later, by the sudden damp chill at her chest.

She opened her red-rimmed eyes slowly, as one hand rose to touch her breasts.

They were leaking milk again.

Ida forced herself to sit up. She opened her dress and began to pump them by hand.

The sudden squeal of the door being thrown opened, the sudden powerful burst of sunlight made Ida fall back in agony.

She balled herself up as tightly as she

could, tried to hide the moisture.

Rough hands were upon her forearms, forcing her to stand. The light was so bright to her dark accustomed eyes that she had to wince for a time before the outside world came into focus.

Ankhesenpaaten was there, staring at her in disbelief.

Ida could see it in her eyes.

She knew.

Ida silently pled with the other woman to hold her peace, her head shaking slowly.

Ankhesenamun's disbelief gave way to jealousy. A slow smile began to form on her lips.

Ida knew then, beyond a shadow of a doubt. Ankhe would tell Horemheb.

As if sensing his name in the women's thoughts, Horemheb appeared at the main gate of the dungeon.

"She has borne a child," the queen proudly announced.

Horemheb entered the cell, shouldered past Ankhe.

He went to Ida and tore aside her dress. He stared in comprehension at the faint stretch marks that marred the perfect flesh of her stomach, at her engorged breasts which even now leaked milk. He let the material go.

He looked at Ankhe, a look of distaste upon his face. "Are you really so hateful that you would lead your very enemy to what could possibly be the only living child of your dead brother?"

He shook his head. "In sealing the fate of Idamun and her child, you have sealed your own. I will not have such a monster loose in my kingdom."

Ankhe stepped back from him.

"Guards!" he called.

Two men stepped forward.

"Take her out into the desert," he ordered. "Make sure no one ever finds her."

A grin of satisfaction played on Ankhesenamun's lips.

The men nodded and moved towards Ida.

"No," Horemheb said gesturing to Ankhe, "Her."

They took Ankhesenpaaten into their custody.

"Wait!" she called as they dragged her away. "You can not do this! I am Queen!"

Ankhe's voice gradually faded until her words were no longer comprehensible.

Once again in silence, Horemheb's attention returned to Ida. "So. Did the boy's seed finally flower or is some other buck to blame?"

"The child is not Pharaoh's," she lied.

Horemheb studied her for a long moment. "Somehow, Ida, I just can't quite bring myself to believe you."

"Grand Vizer, please-"

Horemheb smirked. "Ah, so *now* I have your respect?"

"My child has *nothing* to do with any of you or any of this."

"Perhaps not, but it's always better to be safe than sorry, is it not? Make no mistake, girl. I *will* find you and Tutankhamun's or whoever the hell's bastard and when I do, I will pluck its little heart from its chest and serve it to you for supper."

"Please, no!" Ida sobbed.

"Perhaps we should start in the Land of the Hittites?" he said. "Hattusa, perchance?"

He nodded. "Yes, we'll start there."

He turned to his men. "Take her back to the holding cell," he ordered.

"No!" Ida cried, struggling every step of the way.

The guards did as they were bade, Horemheb following behind them.

Once she was locked in her cell, he spoke loudly enough for her to hear his every word, his sly eyes watching for any reaction.

"Handpick some men and join Ay's next caravan to Hattusa," Horemheb said. "Your presence should be unmarked as such.

"Once you are there, discretely check out every member of Mursili's court - from the slaves to the members of his personal guard, everyone. Do not return until the child is found."

"Hattusa?" one of the men asked. "Why would Pharaoh be going to Hattusa?"

"Because Mursili is trying to broker a peace treaty with him."

"Mursili?" Ida breathed.

Horemheb turned his full attention to Ida. He studied her intensely.

"Know him personally do you?" Horemheb asked.

"No," Ida lied.

"Wasn't he killed?" one of Horemheb's

men asked another. "By Man...Man-"

"Manapa," Horemheb supplied, turning back to face the men.

"Yeah, that's him," another of the soldiers said.

"It would seem this Mursili is more clever than even I had originally imagined," Horemheb replied. "It was he himself who spread the rumor of his untimely defeat.

"Then, soon as Manapa let his guard down, wham! He crushes Manapa and his forces."

Horemheb and his men chuckled.

Horemheb continued. "Word is, when the time came to pay the piper, Manapa sent his own mother out to Mursili to beg forgiveness and to ask that Mursili accept him once more as a vassal of his state.

"Imagine that!"

The men broke into hardy laughter.

"The old bag was even said to grovel right there at Mursili's feet - prostrated and everything!" Horemheb added.

"Mursili, feeling sorry for the old biddy, shows them mercy," Horemheb concluded. "I, on the other hand, would have laughed myself to death and then, beheaded them both!"

Ida sank to the ground and sobbed in her relief. If Mursili was still alive, there might still be hope for her son.

XIX

The days seemed endless as Idaten rotted away in her cell. She could barely eat or sleep. Hope was the only thing keeping her alive. Hope that Horemheb would never find her son.

In the weeks that passed, she had grown gaunt, horrifyingly thin. Her once glorious mane was now wiry.

Every time the door to the dungeons opened, her heart stopped.

Every time she held her breath.

Every time nothing.

She tried to convince herself that Horemheb would never find her son. And though, with each passing day, it seemed more likely he would not, she could not let herself believe it.

Horemheb was relentless, an unstoppable, omnipotent force.

Then the day had come.

Ida had grown so weak that she could hardly rise from her bed anymore. Not that she had any reason to.

It had been the middle of the night when they had roused her, supported her as they led her to one of the side torture chambers.

Horemheb was there. He looked down at her, smiled.

Rather than torture, he had a journey in mind. They set out into the deep desert.

It was cold and inspite of the wraps she wore, she could not keep herself from shivering violently.

They came now to a small cave.

One of the men dismounted her and half-carried her inside. He let her go, leaving her to fall to the ground like a broken puppet.

It was so dark inside that Ida could see nothing. She could only hear the sound of the soldier's footsteps as he walked away.

She began to feel her way along the floor, stopping only when she felt something soft and damp just in front of her.

Her heart stopped in her chest.

Suddenly, a flood of lantern light illuminated the darkness. Ida shielded her eyes against the sudden brightness.

To her horror, the soldiers were walling her up in the cave.

She looked back before her, began screaming hysterically.

There, in the center of the floor, was a tiny body. The face had been bashed in - to the point of being unrecognizable. The tiny heart lay crushed in the dirt next to the corpse. On a gold chain around the child's neck was the pin that Tutankh had given her.

"No!" she screamed over and over again.

"No!" she cried as she let her head fall to rest upon the tiny, empty chest.

She screamed like a mad woman with all of the grief that overwhelmed her heart. Not only had they murdered the child, but they had ensured it would not be able to pass on to the next world.

"I curse you, Horemheb!" she yelled. "Your line shall die with you!"

Horemheb laughed. "I have a healthy wife. Soon, when I am Pharaoh, I shall have dozens more."

"Your line shall die with you!" she repeated.

She turned her attention back to the

child. "Oh, Aten," she sighed taking the lifeless body into her arms and pressing it to her chest. "Oh, god."

XX

Ida thought she was dead at first.

By the time she realized she was neither dead nor hallucinating, a single, thin ray of sunlight had broken through the wall Horemheb's men had built at the mouth of the cave.

The pin was still clutched in her fist, her head still lying on the child's chest as she watched the gap become larger and larger, as she watched brown hands pulling the stones from the entry.

When the hole was large enough, Galeno climbed through and hurried to her side.

"Ida?" he whispered.

She did not answer. She simply stared at him.

He said something loudly in Bedouin. Two of the desert dwellers climbed through the hole and came to Galeno's side.

The men tried to lift her. She would not, however, let go of the dead child.

Galeno finally had to pry her fingers loose, all the while promising to see the child properly buried.

It was all like a dream to Ida. Nothing made any sense. Everything seemed surreal, to be moving in slow motion.

The world tilted, then Ida was still.

Epilogue

"My Queen?" Tuya's personal attendant asked, concerned. She had been awaiting audience with the queen for quite some time now, had at last entered the Queen's chamber without her acknowledgement.

Queen Tuya looked up at the girl, her cheeks streaked with tears.

"Is everything alright?" the girl asked.

Tuya nodded absently. Remembering herself, she wiped away her tears with the back of her hand.

She placed the scrolls on the table back into the chest and locked it. She placed the key around her neck.

Still, even now, she stared at the chest as though she contemplated re-opening it.

"Forgive me, My Queen," the girl gently pressed, "but Pharaoh awaits."

The Queen nodded. "As you will," she said.

The girl bowed to her, then she went to

the antechamber and commanded the rest of the Queen's attendants to enter.

Even as they prepared her, Tuya's thoughts remained upon the scrolls.

If it had been anyone else's audience, she would have postponed them. But this was Ramesses, her son, and he needed her.

Even as she left the room, she made herself and her father a vow.

As soon as she was able, she would return to the scrolls.

Next Read:

**Amarna Book II:
Book of Hawara**

How True is Amarna Book I: Book of Ida?

Okay, this is all being done by memory of research done decades ago. It's as accurate as I can make it without trying to dig up said research.

- The only people who did not specifically exist in reality (though they can be said to be composites of real people) are all of the non-royals and one royal.
- The actual personalities of the Egyptian royals are unknown (except for Akhenaten who left behind lots of clues). I used creative license in a way that I believe supports their known actions (with the except of Ankhe who I just had a bit of fun with).
- A LOT is known about Mursili II, however, as the Hittites were fastidious chroniclers – especially Mursili II himself.
- There really were scandals involving the accusation that priests were engaging in necrophilia -hence Ida waking up with the priest on top of her.
- It was not uncommon for successors to "erase" previous rulers/lines by erasing their names from written history and destroying or reclaiming their deeds/monuments. Ay and Horemheb

were particularly determined to erase the Amarna.

- Ironically, it is believed that Tutankh's tomb was found so intact because one of his successors usurped his intended royal tomb. This means that Aye and Horemheb helped PRESERVE and renew interest in the Amarna (particularly "The Heretic King" and his line) instead of erasing it. Just think about it. How many people have heard of Ay and Horemheb vs. the people who have heard of "King Tut", Nefertiti (his mother) and his father, "The Heretic King" (Akhenaten)?

- Mandrake really was believed to be an ancient aphrodisiac. It was also believed by some to grow as a result of the release of semen, urine and/or blood into the ground by executed criminals at the time of death.

- The penalty for adultery really ranged from having your ears or nose cut off, public flogging, banishment, burning at the stake or being fed to wild animals.

- Beer and other alcohol was often drank more than water (by those who could afford it) as water quality was often not the greatest.

- Egyptians really did wear wigs - some even shaving EVERY HAIR off of their entire body.

- Royal wives really were given a pendant engraved with their and Pharaoh's name.
- It was not uncommon practice in the ancient world for victors to take members of the vanquished ruler's family/household and "adopt" them or put them into service in their household in order to prevent retaliation/rebellion or in order to further subjugate and/or humiliate the defeated – hence Batau and Ida both being of royal blood though slaves.
- The only royal in the book who did not exist in real life? Lord Bietek.
- Akhenaten (Tutankh's and Ankhe's father) was a monotheist. He moved the capital to El-Amarna and took away much of the money and power from polytheists and their priesthood. This did not make him or his many friends.
- Ankhe, Tutankh and others from Akhenaten's household all originally had names that ended in -aten which basically dedicates them to Akhenaten's mono-theistic god, Aten.
- After Akhenaten's death, (various "advisors" and interim rulers) moved the capital back to Thebes, reinstated polytheism and changed the endings of all names to -amun (which rededicates them to the god Amun.
- Tutankh was a child when he became Pharaoh. It is likely that most of that which

was implemented by him as Pharaoh was actually implemented through Any's machinations.

- Ankhe was indeed impregnated by her father Akhenaten. Their resulting daughter was her only surviving child.
- Ankhe also married her brother, Tutankh, who was a young child at the time (and who may have been the son of their father's sister AKA their aunt).
- Tutankh, however, was believed to be in his late teens – somewhere between 17-19 when he died.
- Ankhe is believed to have given birth to two children fathered by Tutankh – both girls and both who died shortly after birth/in the womb.
- Ay was largely credited with "helping" Tutankh to rule once Tutankh was coronated Pharaoh.
- That is until Tutankh was claimed to have mysteriously died after a fall from a chariot in his late teens.
- Originally it was believed that Tutankh was murdered due to the extent and placement of damage to his skull.
- Later forensics has disputed the assassination theory.
- I, however, don't place much faith in forensics conducted thousands of years after the fact (and some days after in some

cases thanks to all of the contamination/falsification scandals).

- If you think about it, Ay is doing what he wants, having a grand old time. Then Tutankh hits puberty. What happens when kids hit puberty? As my father would say, they start smelling the musk under their arms. A Tutankh on the verge of adulthood might have been a lot more difficult to control than Tutankh the child. Especially considering his controversial upbringing in monotheism, it is not inconceivable that perhaps he was starting to allude to Akhenaten-like beliefs or otherwise trying to assert his authority and that Ay, Horemheb or others might have wanted him gone.

- After Tutankh's death, Ankhe really did send a messenger to the Hittites seeking a marriage to one of King Suppiluliuma's sons in order to keep hold of the throne. I chose to make that messenger my fictional character Ida (who was secretly carrying Tutankh's child).

- Suppilu was a real King and a character in and of himself. He murdered his own brother to get the throne (against the law).

- Suppilu also exiled Mursili's mother to marry what some scholars describe as a Babylonian princess in order to solidify/increase his power.

- Some believe the Babylonian princess Suppilu married was Mal-Nikal. (Yes, she was real). Some believe Mal-Nikal was the wife of one of Suppilu's sons. As remarriages between fathers, sons, brothers, siblings, etc. was NOT uncommon amongst royalty and throughout the ancient world, I decided to make Mal-Nikal both.
- After verifying Tutankh was really dead, Suppilu sent one of his sons, Zannanza to marry Ankhe and take over the Egyptian throne.
- Zannanza, however would never make it to Egypt. He was murdered in route.
- While it could be argued it was because the Egyptians did not want to see a Hittite on the Egyptian throne, it could also be argued that Ay and company were wrapping up Operation Usurper.
- Lord Bietek is a composite of all of the royals who objected to Ay and Horemheb's succession. Such a person would likely help hide someone he believed could dethrone them.
- There was frequently tension between Upper and Lower Egypt – particularly after Tutankh's death. At times Upper and Lower Egypt were even ruled by separate kings. The famous Egyptian double crown represents Upper Egypt and Lower Egypt combined under the same rule.

- After the so called Zannanza Affair, Ankhe married Ay. This gave Ay's claim to the throne some legitimacy (though many were not happy about his succession).
- Ankhe disappears from history sometime after this marriage and before Horemheb ascends the throne.
- Ankhe's daughter with Akhenaten disappears from history sometime after Tutankh's death.
- What actually happened to both females is a mystery.
- Ay's connection to the Amarnas is controversial. Some believe him to be of some blood connection to the Amarnas or at least to royalty. Some think not.
- Horemheb's accession, on the other hand, was the most controversial as he was NOT noble.
- However, Horemheb controlled the military.
- Suppilu was very angry and upset by his son's murder. He sent missives to Egypt demanding explanation for this betrayal.
- Egypt didn't even bother to respond.
- Suppilu decided to teach Egypt a lesson. He consulted the oracles who told him NOT to invade Egypt.
- Suppilu ignored the oracle and invaded Egypt anyway.

- Though Suppilu succeeded on a military level, he ended up bring back plague to Hattusa (via Egyptian prisoners) – a plague that ended up killing both him and his successor.
- A famine also devastated Hattusa at the same time as the plague.
- Mursili II wrote what can be considered one of the 1st known personal diaries/autobiographies in history. Much about the events after Tutankh's death and in Hattusa at the time comes from his first-hand accounts.
- Deeply religious, Mursili II believed that all of these actions on the part of his father Suppilu (from the murder of his brother to ignoring the oracle and invading Egypt) was the cause of all of the misfortunes that plagued the Hittite Empire.
- As a result, Mursili became obsessed with appeasing the gods – specifically his patron gods: Telipinu and Arinna.
- Mursili also believed he could actually commune with these gods. This led me to make him a psychic who had inherited it from his banished mother.
- Mursili was known for being fairly tolerant of other's beliefs and reasonably fair.
- Mursili II really was NEVER expected to ascend to the throne, yet a series of unexpected events catapulted him to power as a teen.

- Many of the Hittite vassals DID rebel as they figured the teen could not stop them.
- Brothers Arnuwanda and Mursili's conflict over Ida, however, was added for dramatic effect as Ida isn't real.
- Mursili proved his doubters wrong. He WAS a great warrior, strategist and king.
- However, Mursili's loved ones really DID drop like flies around him – and for the causes as described in the books.
- Mursili DID fake his own death to lull rebelling states into a sense of complacency.
- The account of a vanquished rebel vassal sending out his mother to plead with Mursili is TRUE.
- And Mursili actually DID take pity on him.

A Word from the Author

Did you enjoy this title?

Well of course you did! Why else would you be reading these words right now? (Note: Any other reason aside from the continued joy Grea brings into your life might result in the application of a restraining order and/or institutionalization.)

If you're interested in seeing what else I might have banging about in my brain, please take a moment to review. Reviews are the lifeblood of little ol' independent writers such as myself. The more reviews I get, the more readers I attract and the more deeply I am able to contaminate...er, infest...um, penetrate the literary world.

What does this mean for you, you ask? It means I will write MORE. I will publish MORE....and I won't hunt you down like the naughty little SeaMonkey you are, hog tie you and shame you in the public square.

See? Everybody wins! Yay us!

I know. I know. It's scary using your words; but rest assured, your words don't have to be Shakespearean or in the format of a college entrance essay. Just a sentence or two with your honest review will suffice. However, if you are bard-esque or scored at least a rating equivalent to Good or Above Average on your college entry essay, please feel free to pontificate.

As it would take up too much time and space to list links to everywhere you could possibly buy my books/post your review, click here for direct links to my work on known SeaMonkey Ink retailers: http://seamonkeyink.com/smi_indexes_2013_0 13.htm or simply go back to the site from which you got the book.

Additionally, you may like to publish your review here (or anywhere else you publish reviews):

Goodreads
http://www.goodreads.com/GreaAlexander
LibraryThing
https://www.librarything.com/author/alexanderg rea

Thank you in advance for your kind and completely un-coerced cooperation.

Your awesomeness precedes you.

Grea.

Coming Soon:

Amarna Book II:
Book of Hawara

**Also look for these upcoming titles from
Grea Alexander & SeaMonkey Ink,
LLC:**

Cabello Book I: The Beginning

M

Aberration: Esau

The Pack Book I: Addison

Rebellion Book I: Book of Quay

Rebellion Book II: Book of Soung

Rebellion Book III: Book of Choi

The Pack Book II: Bristol

Cabello Book II: Descendant

Sedition Book I: Book of Xian

Made in the USA
Monee, IL
29 April 2021